MW01124489

Winging It

Cody's Cowboys Save the Day

By
Richard Hamilton

authorHOUSE™

1663 LIBERTY DRIVE, SUITE 200
BLOOMINGTON, INDIANA 47403
(800) 839-8640
WWW.AUTHORHOUSE.COM

First published by AuthorHouse 11/21/05

ISBN: 1-4208-8373-9 (sc)
ISBN: 1-4208-8374-7 (dj)

Printed in the United States of America
Bloomington, Indiana

This book is printed on acid-free paper.

Many thanks to Peter Teichman at Hangar 11 Essex UK for the G-BRVE Photographs

I dedicate this book to Dana, Mark, and the others who are fascinated with the sky; the ones who watch the birds as they soar through the open space above with envy and yearn to investigate the clouds. They always notice the contrails left by the planes flying high above and wonder how it would feel to be the pilot.

I hope they dare to follow their dreams.

Best Wishes

- Richd Hamilton

CHAPTER ONE

The sun was setting when I heard Mom's call, "Eddie, time for dinner."

"Coming Mom," I hollered. "Hey, fumble-fingers, try to catch this one." I burned a hard fastball to my best friend, Jack Davis. Nut's he caught it.

Jack tossed the baseball in the air, smiling his head off. "You throw like a girl, noodle-arm. Is that the best you've got?"

"You were just lucky," I yelled as I turned for the house.

"Don't forget to pad your mitt tomorrow, noodle-arm. I'll show you a real fast-ball."

"Yeah, yeah," I said. "See ya."

As I approached the door, my dog, Andy, a six-year old miniature schnauzer, greeted me. We wrestled around on the grass for a little while. He loves to play.

"Eddie!"

"Come on, Andy—time to eat. Hey Mom," I shouted as I entered the house, almost falling to keep the screen door from slamming. Phew, caught it, Mom was mad enough. "Do I have time to feed Andy? He's giving me that starving look; I don't think he can wait."

"Okay, honey, but <u>hurry</u>, I don't want the dinner to get cold. Jim! Dinners on."

I hurried to the laundry room where Andy ate. I measured out a cup of dog food, added some hot water, and placed it in front of the circling Andy. "Here you go, big boy." He dug in. "Why do you always circle to the right when you get excited? Did someone hit your head or something when you were a puppy—before we rescued you from the pound? That's it, ignore me now that you got your food—and quit wagging your tail, I know you're happy."

"Eddie—<u>Now</u>!"

"Yeah, Mom." Oops, I had better wash my hands or she will kill me. I retreated to the bathroom and rinsed off most of the dirt, taking the towel with me on the way to the kitchen. I tossed the muddy towel on the counter and got that exasperated look. "Sorry, I had to hurry didn't I?" I stopped by my chair for a minute to check out what Mom had fixed. "Oh boy, fried chicken and mashed potatoes—my favorite," I said, leaning over the table to get a whiff. This time the look came from Dad.

I quickly sat down and whisked the napkin off my plate. Then, Dad started saying the grace. "*God is good, God is grace; Let us thank him for our food. By his hand we all are fed; Give us Lord our daily bread."* Amen, we all said in unison.

Mom served up. Everyone had to have full plates before you could start eating, a rule in our house. Finally, we began. Mmmm. I had to hand it to Mom; she could cook—not just chicken—everything she fixed—except for broccoli, ugh. The meal went quickly as we all liked chicken.

Mom had just started serving dessert, some leftover brownies, when Dad interrupted, "Sit down a minute, honey, I have some news that affects us all." Oh no, here he goes again. Why does he always interrupt dessert with a speech? "There's no easy way to say this, so here goes— I've been transferred." Silence filled the room. I reached for a brownie and got a slap on the hand from Mom.

Dad continued, "I had no idea, no warning. I was completely surprised. Bill caught me just as I was leaving the office. He said the Agency needs a senior Gulfstream pilot in Laredo, Texas, and I am it. The program has a super high priority, requested by the President." Dad sighed, then added, "I guess there's some serious smuggling going on across the border in the south Texas area that has National interest— White House interest."

Mom just sat there, then put her hands over her ears as she does sometimes, meaning she didn't want to hear anymore. "It will mean a promotion," Dad said quickly, looking a bit desperate for a positive response. "I'm sorry, Janet, I really don't have any choice."

I was still eyeing a brownie when the news sunk in. Moving! Does he mean leaving here for good? Oh my gosh!

My mouth was still open when Mom spoke, doing her best to accept what he said. Oh man, she's going to cry. I hated that. "I understand, Jim, it's just tough—you know." She bit her lip, and tears were running down her face. "When do we have to leave? Can we all go together?" She wiped her eyes with her napkin. Poor Mom, she always takes things so hard.

Dad stood up and started pacing. Here we go again—more lecture. "I'm not sure. I don't know any of the details yet, but I'm afraid that I will have to report immediately. Then you and Eddie can join me after school is out. All I know is the new program is permanent—not just a short-term assignment. I hate to break it to you like this, honey—aaah nuts!" Mom jumped up and they hugged.

They were too busy to notice, so I snagged a couple of brownies and left for my bedroom. It was only now that the news really, **really**, sunk in. My life was over.

I jumped on my bed and just laid there in the dark, nibbling on a brownie. Andy joined me and snuggled up by my side, showing little interested in my dessert. I wondered if he knew. He must, I decided, otherwise he'd be begging.

I quickly switched on the light and found my atlas. Where in the world is Laredo? I finally found it. Oh no, it was located right on the Rio Grande River in the southernmost part of Texas—practically in Mexico. The city was only a little bitty dot on the map, not half as big as Homestead, Florida. What am I in for? What about school? What about my friends? Don't they care about me? It was a disaster, all right! Yes, my life was over.

"Eddie! Have you done your homework? I'll want to see it in the morning." Andy groaned loudly when I moved to get my backpack—he must have known that his life was over too.

"I'm doin it now, Mom." I read part of my history assignment—boring, and finished a math paper—math was easy for me. I decided to hold off working on my science project, I wasn't in the mood for heavy thinking. Besides, I had already downloaded a bunch of stuff from the internet and had most everything I needed—and I had almost a month before I would have to give my presentation.

I wandered out to the kitchen to see if there were any more brownies—there weren't. The kitchen was clean as a pin. Poor Mom, she always needed to clean stuff when she was upset. She and Dad would both be in the den watching TV, neither of them saying a word to each other. They always acted that way after one of their 'discussions.' They'd wait until they were in bed and then talk half the night away. Sometimes parents are weird.

I turned in about nine-thirty. Andy growled menacingly when I moved him from my pillow to his. Every night he did the same thing. Boy is he spoiled. I yawned, Andy joined me,—we were both pretty beat. It had been a tough day.

———————————

I woke up hearing voices—my folks were talking. My clock said eleven. I yawned, but decided against closing my window—this night I wanted to hear what they had to say. I slipped off the screen, crawled out of the window, and sat down under theirs. Their window was only about six feet from mine and their bed was close to it. I'm sure they didn't know I could hear them.

Dad was talking up a storm, as usual, explaining everything in detail: the responsibilities of his new job, selling our house, finding a new place in Laredo, and coming back to help Mom move. That's not what Mom wanted to hear. Me neither, I was freezing—get on with it, Dad.

Mom finally got her chance. "I'm worried more about Eddie than I am about the move. He had almost been in the same school for all of his life, and it will kill him to lose Jack, they're so close. And it's such a tough age to make new friends. It could even affect his school work."

"Sweetheart. Janet. Please! Don't worry about Eddie. He'll get over it, he's not a little kid anymore, and he'll be almost thirteen when he starts the eighth grade. We both had to move when we were young. It didn't hurt us did it?" He quieted down. I could tell Mom was glaring at him.

Her voice sounded kind of stern. "That's why I wanted you to get out of the Air Force, Jim. Don't you remember? You were never home, and we moved three times before Eddie was seven."

"I got out of the Air Force just like you wanted, and we've been here close to six years. That's stable if you ask me. You knew what I was getting into when I joined this flying program for the CIA. Hell, I'm lucky. Most of my counterparts have moved way more than us."

"You never seem to really understand, Jim." Mom's voice sounded mad, real quiet, but mad. I hated to hear my folks argue. It would be tough living with them for the next couple of days. Shivering, I climbed back in, fixed the screen, and closed the window. I jumped on the bed, covered up, and buried my head in my pillow. Andy snuggled up again. I gave him a quick tummy rub—at least I'd have him.

———————————

Knock. Knock. Mom opened the door a smidgen. "Eddie, time to get up. Breakfast is almost ready."

"Yeah, Mom. Come on, Andy, get up." Andy smushed down in his pillow, holding his eyes tightly closed. "Hungry? It's Numma-num time, big boy." Andy stirred at the sound of food, then sleepily jumped off the bed and stretched. I hurriedly made my bed, knowing that Mom would inspect the room while I ate breakfast and make me come back and to do it anyway. I pulled on my jeans and slipped on a clean tee shirt, hiding the dirty one under my pillow. "Come on, Andy."

"Eddie."

"I'm feeding Andy."

"Don't forget to brush your teeth." I walked back to the bathroom and brushed my teeth. For good measure, I splashed my face with water just in case she checked me out.

I went to the kitchen and sat down. "Morning, Mom."

"Don't I get a kiss?" She came over and gave me a smack on the cheek, then tried to slick back my hair. "Did you sleep well?"

"Okay, I guess. Where's Dad?"

"He went to work early." Her voice was curt, so I decided not to mention Dad again. "I want you to put the trash out before you go, and don't forget to put a twist-tie on the top. I want to see your homework too."

"Yes, Mom." After I gulped down my glass of orange juice, I started eating my Cheerios and banana, saving the toast and jelly for last.

"Don't eat so fast, Eddie. You'll get indigestion."

"Yes, Mom." She disappeared. Probably checking to see if I made my bed. Andy appeared under the table, begging for a piece of banana. I slipped him one quickly, before Mom came back.

"I'm glad you remembered to make your bed, but I'm tired of you leaving dirty clothes under your pillow. They belong in the laundry room. I don't want to tell you again. Do you understand?

"Yes, Mother." I started on my toast. Mmmm-raspberry jam.

"Yes, Mother what?"

Ah oh, it's going to be one of those mornings. "Yes Mother, I'll put all of my dirty stuff in the laundry room. I won't forget. <u>All-right?</u>"

Suddenly, she kissed me on the cheek again. "I'm sorry, Eddie. I guess I'm upset about having to move."

"That's okay, Mom. I know."

She sat down, having that serious look. "How do you feel about it? Moving, I mean.

Boy, I thought, that's a loaded question. "Heck, I don't know. I don't want to leave here, but I guess I have to. What choice do I have?" Her face was getting red, and I didn't want her to start crying. "It's okay with me, Mom, Really," I lied, quickly changing the subject. "I'd better get going with the trash and stuff, or I'll miss the bus." She hugged me when I got up, and busied herself with the dishes. "Do you want to see my homework?" She shook her head no, fighting off tears. I donned my backpack and headed for the garage to get the trash. I hated it when Mom was upset, and what I said didn't help—she always seemed to know when I lied.

CHAPTER TWO

Jack whistled loudly from the corner where the bus stopped, and was jumping up and down like an idiot—almost tripping on his cuffs because he was wearing those stupid low-hanging pants. "Hurry up, noodle-arm, the bus is coming."

"Oh yeah. You were lucky to catch it, fumble-fingers," I yelled, "What'd you do? Put glue on your glove?" I ran for the last little bit and arrived at the curb just as the bus came screeching to a stop—smoke was billowing from the exhaust. I wondered why they put the tail-pipe next to the door; it should be at the back. I fell in behind Jack and scurried up the doorway stairs. We were dead last, and had to fight our way through a bunch of giggling girls to the back seat where we always sat. Riding the bus was such a hassle.

Jack spoke first. "Why were you late? You forget the trash again?"

"It's a long story. I don't want to talk about it."

"Are you in trouble with your folks? What'd you do this time? It must have been more than just the trash. Did you sass your Dad or something?"

"No! It's way worse than that."

"Worse! Wow! What is it?"

"We're moving to Texas."

Jack just sat there for a minute—kind of stunned. "You mean you're leaving Homestead? For good?" I nodded. "But you can't. What will I do when you leave? Who will I hang around with?" He let his backpack fall to the floor and held his hands on his head. "Are you sure? Are you kidding me?" He turned and gave me a big grin. "That's it, you're teasing." Then he saw my look. "Oh, No. It's true, isn't it? How could you do this to me, Eddie? I'm supposed to be your best friend."

I pretended like he didn't say all that stuff. After all, I didn't want to make him think he was a sissy or something for talking about how he felt. Once, I tried to make him forget by kicking the seat in front of me, to get the kids sitting there to start throwing spitballs or something. It didn't work. Must be a couple of wimps, I figured. We rode in silence until we arrived at school. "Let's use the emergency exit," I suggested, hoping that might kick up a little excitement. "Come on, I don't want to listen to those girls again."

"We'll get in trouble, Eddie. Don't you remember the last time? We had to talk to the Vice Principal. He said we'd get paddled if we did it again."

"I don't care."

"Well I care. I'm the one who'll suffer the consequences, not you. I'll still be here after you go," he said, still trying to get even for my leaving.

"Okay," I said. "Let's just wait until everyone gets off." We just sat there. Boy, he was in bad shape. I really felt guilty. I don't know why but I did. After all, I wasn't the one who decided to leave.

————————————

Suddenly the driver shouted. "Are you guys going to get off, or are you going to the garage with me?"

"We're leaving," I said, "Come on, Jack, I have to stop by my locker first." Jack must have still been in shock, because he just sat there.

I punched him. "What? Oh yeah, we're here." He picked up his backpack and threw it over his shoulder without even trying to punch me back. Boy, he must be sick.

"Snap out of it, Jack. It's not going to be that bad. Heck, maybe you can come for a visit."

That got him going. "Are you kidding me?" He ran his fingers through his shaggy blond hair. "Why would I ever want to visit Laredo—it's bound to be a dump. Besides, I can't speak Mexican."

"They speak Spanish, you meathead, Mexican's not a language. They speak English there too. It's still in America you know—even if it is Texas."

"Barely," Jack answered. "At least that's what Victoria said, and she's taken Spanish her whole life."

"She said what?"

"That Mexicans don't speak real Spanish. They only do that in Spain, stupid."

"Then Victoria's wrong."

"She's never wrong—she's a brain." I had to admit, he had me there. Victoria was a brain. And not bad looking either, except for her fuzzy hair. We arrived at the door. I turned right and Jack turned left.

The bell rang.

"See ya," We both said.

———————————

I stopped by my locker and picked up the book on astronomy I'd gotten from the library. I would need it for third period science class. Mrs. Williams always wanted to see the book you were using for a science project. My project was about the alignment of five planets: Mercury, Venus, Mars, Jupiter, and Saturn. Our Moon even joins them for a few days. Actually, the Moon wasn't a planet, but it also had a predictable orbit, and that's what I needed to prove my case. Anyway, they were going to align during late April through early May and my neighbor, Mr. Horn, said he would let me look at them through his telescope and take a picture. I was counting on getting a picture of the event—that would get me an A for sure—teachers always liked that personal involvement stuff.

I suffered through Mr. Alford's World History class. Boy, was he boring. All he cared about was dates. Actually, the history part wasn't so bad; it was how he talked about it. He kept me forgetting about the important stuff and only remembering the exact minute things happened.

Math was next: special student beginning Algebra. At least Mrs. Lester was interesting. She explained why the formulas were important and why they worked. I got an A on my homework, naturally, and got to explain how I got problem number three—the only one in the class that did. School could be fun when you were good at something.

Jack caught up with me on the way to Science. "Have you got a project yet? I heard Mrs. Williams wants to get everybody assigned today. Bob said she's trying to get two people to work on every project— to make it more meaningful. Ha, boy is she dumb, if that's what she thinks. Anyway, want to make a volcano with me?"

"A volcano. I did one of those when I was a little kid."

"Yeah. Me too. But it's easy, and she doesn't have to know we did it before."

"I don't know, Jack. I have something else in mind—about astronomy. See. Here's my book. Besides, I've already started—kind of."

"Okay. I don't know anything about that stuff. Maybe Paul will do a volcano with me." The bell rang and we sat down. Mrs. Williams gave us a lecture on how important science projects were—I almost went to sleep.

Then, out of the blue, Mrs. Williams called my name. "Eddie Matthews, let's start with you. What have you chosen to do?"

I jumped up so fast I dropped my book on the floor. Everyone laughed. Red-faced, I picked it up and quickly explained the alignment of planets, then showed them an old picture of when it happened last. All the kids were impressed when I told them it wouldn't happen again until 2040—when we would all be really really old, like fifty something.

Mrs. Williams was also impressed. I guess she was so impressed that she decided I needed help. "Miss Thomas, Victoria, this project seems made to order for you as well. Do you want to join Eddie?"

Wait a minute. I just stood there looking dumb, wondering why she didn't ask me about sharing my idea. I was about to say something when Victoria appeared at my side looking tall and gawky, as usual, her kinky brown hair pulled back in that dumb ponytail—which was bigger than a soccer ball. "I'd love to, Mrs. Williams," she said grinning, "I think this project was made in heaven." Everyone laughed, until they got the connection and realized how dumb it was. A couple of the guys were giggling and pointing at me. At that point, I was just trying not to be embarrassed.

"Oh, Victoria, you are <u>so</u> quick," Mrs. Williams laughed, "I just know the class will love your presentation." Her presentation? Wait a minute; I thought silently, the presentation was my idea. I thought about strangling Victoria then and there, but sat down instead—I still wanted that A from the teacher.

I was just starting to get over it when the bell rang. Jack immediately came over and started to rag me about Victoria. "Maybe she can teach you Mexican—I mean Spanish. Ha Ha."

I was ready to punch him out when Victoria appeared out of nowhere. "Hi, Eddie. Here's my phone number." I looked puzzled. "So you can call me when your neighbor is going to take us to look at the planets," she continued. "This is going to be so much fun. I'm so excited." That was an understatement; her whole body seemed to grin.

"Ah, Okay," I said, trying to be indifferent. "I was going to ask you later how I could get in touch with you," I added, not knowing exactly why I said it. She gave me a big smile and turned to leave. She whirled around so fast that her ponytail caught me right in the face.

Jack started to laugh after she was gone. "This project was made in heaven," he taunted, then doubled over. I kicked him. The only one that was going to be happy about this situation was Mom.

———————————

The bus trip home after school was much better than the morning ride; at least Jack wasn't so upset about me leaving. I guess he was happy because he got Paul Goggin to do a volcano with him. Sometimes I had to wonder if Jack was actually twelve.

I saw Mr. Horn working in the yard and decided to let him know about Victoria. "Hi, Eddie," he waved as I walked up. "I've been watching the weather channel every night, and decided the perfect time to see the planet alignment is on the fifth of May. That will give us at least a one-week window to catch the event, in case something happens. That okay with you?"

"That seems swell to me, Mr. Horn. By the way, my teacher assigned another student to work with me. Her name is Victoria. Don't worry," I assured him after seeing his reaction, "She's a brain. She won't cause any trouble."

"No problem. I've got plenty of room in the van." He seemed happy about Victoria joining us, and asked me if she was my girl friend—giving me that silly little wink that grown-ups make when they think it will embarrass you.

"No," I said loudly. "Not at all!" I don't think he believed me, and he just went on raking the grass with a big smirk on his face—being sure he'd succeeded in embarrassing me. I took a deep breath to settle my stomach. "See ya, Mr. Horn." He waved, still grinning.

Andy attacked me when I can in the house. As usual, he started circling like crazy and ran for the washroom. "No, Andy. It's too early to eat."

"Eddie. Is that you?"

"Yes, Mom."

"Come in here, quick! I have some good news." I dumped my backpack and hurried to the kitchen. When I walked in, I got a big hug and a kiss from Mom. It must be good news, I figured. She pulled me to the table and sat me down. "Eddie. We are only going to be in Laredo for a maximum of two years. We will be coming back to Homestead—isn't that great? You can attend high school here."

That's good news. What was she thinking about? It's good news that we will only be living at the end of the earth for two years. She seemed so happy though, and I made myself give her a big smile. "Great," I replied, weakly. "Terrific." Boy, I wondered. Just how much of this great news stuff can a guy stand?

She quickly returned to the sink. "I knew you'd be happy. Bet you can't wait to tell Jack. He'll be thrilled."

"Yeah. He'll be happy, all-right." How could she think he'd be happy? He would still be without me for two years.

"Oh," Mom continued, "Dad is going to leave day after tomorrow. He will find us a place to live. I think you and I can move around June 5th, right after school's out. Oh! That's the other good news—we don't have to sell our house."

Now that <u>was</u> good news. I liked our house. I practically grew up here. Good location too. "Did Dad's boss change his mind or something?"

"I guess Bill was so upset about losing your father for good, he threw a fit. We didn't know it, but Bill was planning to have Jim take over the operation here in a couple of years. So, he talked the powers at be into sending Jim to Laredo temporarily, to set up the operation there—to get his feet wet, so to speak, managing a similar operation." She turned, quickly. "Oh. Eddie, honey. Get me two packages of chicken breasts out of the freezer in the garage."

"Sure, Mom." Getting his feet wet is about all he'll get wet in Laredo, I was thinking as I headed for the garage. There's no deep water around there for a zillion miles. It's just about a desert. I found the chicken and was back in a flash. "Here, Mom. Are these the ones?"

"Just what I wanted. Put this one in the fridge, please," she said, handing me back one of the packages. "Isn't it wonderful?" she continued. "We'll be here at least four years after we get back, and you can finish school."

She'd already said that once, but I decided not to say anything. She was almost dancing around the kitchen. At least she was happy again. So much for the big argument last night. Boy, grown ups are strange.

"Eddie! You should have time to do your homework before dinner. Better get started."

"I don't have hardly any homework," I pleaded.

"Well that's good. You will finish all the sooner. Then you can help me with dinner."

"Yes, Mom." Nuts. I should have known better than to tell her I didn't have much homework. She always turns what I say around and cons me into helping her. Man, I've got to learn to think before I say something. I'm to old to fall for that one every time.

Andy and I headed for my room. I turned on my CD player and started reading while he took a nap. I swear that dog must sleep twenty hours a day. The book wasn't bad: The Hobbit. It's about strange little people who live in the middle-earth. I have to read it for Mrs. Edward's English class. It's a little too complicated to explain here, so you'll just have to read it for yourself. Anyway, she's a pretty good teacher and doesn't require you to remember every little detail when you do your book report. I think she mainly wanted us to read a lot of books.

"Eddie, turn down that music, or what ever you call it. It's too loud. I can hear it all the way in here. I know you can't concentrate with all of that noise—you won't be able to hear a thing by the time you grow up."

"Yes, Mom," I said, turning down the CD a bit. I don't know what's wrong with parents; I guess they just don't like music.

After about an hour, Mom called. "Eddie! Time to set the table. Then you can feed Andy."

"Coming, Mom." Andy heard Mom say his name and immediately headed for the laundry room. He seemed really mad when I headed for the kitchen. "Hi, Mom. What dishes do you want me to use?

"The regular pottery and the stainless flatware." She paused and looked at my hair. "I think you need a haircut," she said, trying to pat down my cowlick.

I ducked. "Okay, I'll get the usual stuff." Flatware? I never could figure out why Mom always called knives, forks, and spoons flatware. Why can't she just shorten it to stainless or silver like everyone else does? I finished everything in about ten minutes, and then fed Andy. Dad arrived just as I got home from taking Andy for a walk around the block. "Hey, Dad," I said, giving him a wave.

"Eddie! Please put the rake in the garage."

"Okay, Dad." Boy, don't parents ever just say hello. Why do they always see something for you to do? I put away the rake and pushed down the lid on the trashcan. That made me fume all the more. If he had seen that loose lid, he would probably have gotten me out of bed to fix it. As I headed for the kitchen, I heard Dad talking to Mom. He sounded real serious, so I stood for a moment outside the doorway to get the gist of things.

Dad started. "Bill briefed me about Laredo today."

Mom perked up. "Oh. Really? What's going on?"

"Well, the FBI arrested a terrorist in Dallas last week. I guess he admitted he was smuggled into the States somewhere near Laredo, and was going to set up some kind of operation to handle a new cell located in the Dallas metroplex."

"Wow, Jim. Where is he from?"

"He's a Peruvian, surprisingly. Belongs to a bad-guy-group called, Shining Path. I guess they support al Qaeda and Hammas too. The guy trained in Libya, and he is both a pilot and explosives expert. Bad, huh?"

"That's horrible. Did they fly him in? Is that why you're going?"

"He obviously was flown into Mexico, but they're not sure if he was flown across the border. They may have landed in Mexico first, then brought him in by foot or maybe even by helicopter. That's the reason they want our surveillance bird down there in a hurry. As you know the Gulfstream has the best capabilities in the world for this kind of job."

She stiffened, and her voice got real serious. "Will you be in danger? I mean won't they want to stop your missions? Sabotage the plane or something?"

"We can't be sure, but the Agency's not going to take any chances. They're already beefing up the security at the airfield, and especially around our operations area."

Mom gave Dad a big hug. "Oh, honey. I swear it's always something. I know that you love your country and have always volunteered to protect it—and you've invariably put Eddie and I at the top of your list. I've always been so proud of you for that. I don't want to sound silly or overly concerned, but at the same time, I worry. Do you know what I mean? I don't want Eddie to be afraid that something will happen to his Dad."

Dad grabbed her. "Janet, I'll be fine. We'll all be fine." Then he pushed her back, and looked at her, then gave her a kiss. "I love you, honey. It's okay." She relaxed. Then he said, "How long before dinner? I'm starving."

That broke the spell with Mom. "As soon as I call Eddie," she said, shaking her head. They stood there for a minute, holding each other. That was my clue. I stamped my feet like I was coming down the hall.

"Hi. When do we eat?"

Mom looked at Dad and rolled her eyes. "Like father, like son." She turned her attention to me. "Eddie, have you washed your hands?"

"Oh, man," I said, and rushed back to the bathroom. I swear she never forgets anything.

"Don't just wipe the dirt off on the towel," I heard from the kitchen. Oh, no, she caught me again.

———————————

I read a little more after dinner and then turned in. I got the usual Grrr from Andy when I moved him. I waited for him to build a nest on his pillow and then turned out the light.

I laid there in the dark and thought over what Mom and Dad had said about the job in Laredo. I guess my Dad is pretty patriotic, and I know he's not scared of anything. Heck, he was an Air Force fighter pilot before he went to work for the CIA. Oops! I'm not supposed to say CIA to anyone—just say he worked for a Government Agency. I wonder if it was okay to think, CIA. Anyway, I decided to pay more attention to Dad—about what he did, I mean. Besides, Jack wouldn't be there—and a guy had to have something to think about, didn't he?

That got me to thinking about Jack. I was pretty lucky, compared to him. He only had his mom to take care of him. His dad walked out on them years ago, he told me, but he's never told me much more than that. I don't think Jack even knows what he looks like, or where he lives anymore.

Anyway, his dad never sends them money, and his mom has to work all the time and is never home. I guess she doesn't have time to cook anything good, like Mom does. I think Jack almost lives on pizza. It's too bad, I know how much he eats when he stays over here for dinner—and he talks a lot about how good a cook Mom is. Poor guy, he even gave most of the money we earned mowing lawns last year to his mom.

We never talk about it though, guys just don't do that—even if they're interested. Heck, I wouldn't want to embarrass him by bringing it up. I wonder if he could come and stay with us in Laredo. He'd kick up a fuss, but I know he'd love to come—even if it was just to eat. I decided to ask Mom in the morning.

Feeling better, I puffed up my pillow and went to sleep. I was tired from all that thinking.

CHAPTER THREE

The next morning, I asked Mom if she thought that Jack could come and stay with us for a while in Laredo. "His mom works all the time and he won't have anyone to do stuff with. He might even get into trouble being all by himself," I added, trying to make my case stronger.

Mom stopped dusting. "Why that's a wonderful idea, Eddie. How thoughtful of you. I'll make a point of calling Caroline Davis to see what she thinks about the idea. She told me something about wanting to attend school full time, and this might give her a chance. I'm sure Dad won't mind. He wouldn't want you to get in trouble either, being all by yourself, too." Boy, I marveled, as I left for school, you could not put much over on Mom,—she picked up quick on that 'might get in trouble thing.' Oh well, if anybody can make this thing work it'll be Mom.

The next day at school was pretty quiet. Jack did not say much, so I didn't say much back. I told Victoria about going to look at the planets on the fifth of May. I think she was excited about the project, because she had already studied up on it and knew quite a bit. I decided I'd better bone up too, just in case Mrs. Williams asked us any serious questions. I decided to stop by the library and take another look on the internet for anything I might have missed. I didn't want my new partner to show me up.

When I got home, Mom said she'd talked with Mrs. Davis and seemed pretty sure that Jack could stay with us for most of the summer. Mom said she might even stay in our house until the end of September, which would help with her college finances. Mom said that Dad's friend, who was originally going to rent the house from us, couldn't be their till October. That would work out perfect for everyone. Sounded good to me. Now, all I had to do was convince Jack.

———————————

Jack started off big time, when I met him at the bus stop the next morning. "Why'd you ask my mom if I could stay with you this summer without asking me first?"

I took the tough approach. "Cause I knew you would say no, for some dumb reason or other, and I wanted you to come."

"Well, that's no fair, Eddie. Mom's all excited now, and I can't tell her I don't want to go—it would kill her. Do you realize what you did to me? I'm going to have to live in a crappy place all summer, will have to help move out of our apartment, and put all of my good stuff in storage boxes. Boy, Eddie, that's no fair."

"Sure it's fair," I said, defending the decision, as we climbed on the bus. "Your mom gets to finish school like she wants, and you are going to have the most fun you have ever had."

"Will not."

"Will too." We sat down on the back seat. I punched him. "Sure you will. We can do all sorts of neat stuff together. It will be an adventure."

He punched me back—getting even. "What kind of adventure? Do you think eating beans everyday is an adventure?"

"Who said anything about beans? Mom doesn't cook beans. She makes good stuff—stuff you like." I think I had him there. He was starting to weaken. "We can mess around the airport everyday. Dad said we might be able to get a job at a small flying service there—washing airplanes or something. That should be fun. Have you ever messed around planes?"

Jack thought a minute. "No, but who said that was fun? What kind of adventure is that?"

"I think it's a great adventure, considering we might even get to fly." He perked up when I mentioned flying.

"Really?"

"I'm almost positive," I lied, quickly crossing my fingers.

He got kind of excited. "I've never been in an airplane. I've always wanted to fly."

"Told you it was going to be an adventure," I said, leaning back, knowing I had him.

He punched me when we pulled into the bus stop—getting double even, I guess. "Come on, noodle-arm. Let's play a little catch before the bell rings."

"It's starting to rain, dimwit. We can't play in the rain." I was wondering again if Jack was really twelve—sometimes he acted so young.

"Then let's go put double scotch tape on the girl's chairs, so their dresses will stick when they try to get up. Come on." He ran off like an idiot. It was then and there I knew I was right, he couldn't be twelve.

Heck, I got to thinking, maybe the tape thing would be fun— especially if Victoria fell for it. "Hey, Jack. Wait for me," I hollered.

CHAPTER FOUR

Not too much happened until May. Both Victoria and I had done a lot of homework on the planets. She volunteered to make a giant poster of the planet orbits, showing the earth and all of the other planets alignment on the day we would see them, May 5th. The only thing she didn't know how to explain was the way to compute when it would happen the next time. Actually, it was easy—if you were an math expert like me. So I took that part of the presentation, and made a chart to show how you could figure out where all of the planets were mathematically. Of course, most of the class wouldn't know what I was talking about—but that was okay, Mrs. Williams would understand, and I would get an A.

By the time May 5th arrived, things were in an uproar. Victoria's mom didn't want her to go on the trip all by herself—I mean with only Mr. Horn and me. I guess she wanted to make sure her daughter wasn't murdered or anything. Mom kind of agreed with her. I don't know why mothers think we need so much protection; after all, we weren't kids anymore. Besides, Mr. Horn was a neat guy.

Mrs. Thomas and Mom were on the phone for two days. Mom even had her over to meet Mr. Horn, but that wasn't enough. "What's wrong with Mrs. Thomas?" I asked Mom, after another one of her calls. "Don't you guys trust Mr. Horn to take us?"

"Of course we trust him to be with you. It's not that at all. It's just the fact that you are going to a wilderness area at night. Neither of you have had any experience in the everglades. It can be really scary out there. Grown men disappear out there all the time."

I answered her quickly. "But Mr. Horn knows all about the swamp. He's fished there for a hundred years—and we aren't really going into the swamp, we'll just be on the edge."

"We both know that now, after talking with Mr. Horn—and he has assured us that he won't take any chances. As a matter of fact, he suggested that you take cell phones with you, so you could call us if something unforeseen happened. I think it's a good idea—so does Beverly. As a matter of fact, he even gave us a map."

I thought the whole thing was stupid, but I kind of understood—Victoria being a girl and everything. "Well, I guess it's okay. I just didn't want her to be embarrassed or something."

Finally, Mrs. Thomas and Mom seemed satisfied. At least Victoria and I would get to ride out there without our moms tagging along.

I kind of think Mr. Horn understood our predicament, because he winked at me after they agreed.

At last, it was time. I was starting to be glad it was almost over—with all of the uproar our moms were making. Victoria and her mom got there about seven-twenty. Victoria had on Levi's, a sweatshirt, and heavy boots. "What a good idea, Beverly," Mom said, after seeing Victoria's boots. "Eddie, go put on your boots, too. Then you won't have to worry so much about snakes."

Snakes! Now why in the world did she have to mention that? Man, Mrs. Thomas's eyes just about jumped out of her head. "Uh, are there a lot of snakes in that area, Janet?" she said weakly. Oh, Boy. I just knew she'd be upset.

I looked at Victoria. She shrugged her shoulders, and then spoke up quickly. "Not this time of year, Mom. It's too cold." Whew, just in the nick of time. I had to hand it to Victoria; she was quick—just like Mrs. Williams said.

Mrs. Thomas exhaled. "Good. But it doesn't hurt to be safe. Right, Janet?"

"Right, Beverly," she answered. But I could tell Mom hadn't really given much thought about snakes either.

Mr. Horn knocked on the door at seven-thirty on the button. "Good evening, Ladies." He touched the bill of his ball cap as he nodded to our moms. "Come on, you two. We don't want to take all night. I want to be back before ten."

I grabbed my boots and headed for the door. "Let's go, Victoria. Don't worry," I added, turning to both moms'. "I'll make sure we check-in—if there are any problems."

Victoria turned to her mom, after rolling her eyes. "See ya, we'll be fine."

With that, we left and joined Mr. Horn, who had already started his van. "Let's hit the road, you two," he said, as he gunned off. "I never thought we were going to get out of there."

We grinned at each other when we buckled our seatbelts. "Me neither, Mr. Horn," I replied. Victoria nodded, and faked wiping sweat off her brow. Right then and there, I was happy that we were on the project together—she could be pretty fun sometimes. Still, that didn't make her any shorter. Maybe it was just her tall hair, I thought, we'd be about the same height if you smushed down on her fuzzy hair.

We arrived at our spot in about forty minutes. It was a closed down bait-house on the edge of the everglades. Boy was it dark. There were lots of bug noises and some from other critters. I had to admit, it was kind of scary. I mean it was <u>black</u>, and it didn't smell real great either. Mr. Horn left the headlights on so we could see. Then he got his telescope out of the back and carried it over to a spot by the edge of an old beat-up dock. "Hey, Eddie. Go get that garden hose out of the back of the van, will ya?"

"Sure, Mr. Horn." I found it right where he said, about fifty feet of it. "What do you want me to with this hose?" I asked when I returned.

"Oh. Just make a big circle around the scope, here. Use it all, and make sure the ends are screwed together when you get it all spread out."

"What's it for?" I asked a bit puzzled.

"To keep the snakes away while we're looking at the sky. Those moccasins can sneak up on you in the dark. That's all we need is one of you guys to get bit. For some reason those snakes won't cross a hose." He quickly added. "Watch out while you are laying it out, though. If you see a stick about three feet long, it probably ain't a stick. Ha. Ha."

Mr. Fowley, my science teacher last year, said that ropes or hoses don't work with snakes, but I decided it was a good idea to believe Mr. Horn right now. After all, we sure didn't want some big old snake attacking us while we were looking through the telescope.

Suddenly, Victoria was by my side. I gave her a quick elbow to the ribs. "I thought you said it was too cold for snakes."

She shrugged. "I just said that to satisfy my Mom. Heck, I don't know anything about snakes." She jumped a bit after she said it, causing me to take a quick look around.

About the time I got the hose laid out, I heard a big grunting sound. It was followed by a bunch of others, coming from everywhere around us. They seemed to be getting louder. I looked at Mr. Horn. "Gators," he said, nonchalantly. "If you hear one real close, turn the flashlight on it—they're scared of the light."

Victoria moved over close again. "Don't worry," I told her. "It's just Alligators. They won't hurt you unless you get too close to the water. Besides, you only have to worry about the big ones."

She seemed a little nervous. "How do you know if it's a big one? They all sound about the same."

Mr. Horn came to my rescue. "Those Gators won't hurt you unless you fall on one. "Come on. I'm ready. Eddie, go turn out the headlights. Are you guys ready to see some planets?"

I turned out the lights and couldn't see a thing. Not even my hand. "It's perfect for watching, blacker than a coal mine out here," Mr. Horn hollered, then realized I couldn't see. "Just wait there a minute, Eddie. Your eyes will get used to it."

I waited a minute, and, sure enough, I started to see. I stood by until Victoria finished looking. Then it was my turn. Wow! He had them lined up perfect. Jupiter was on the top, the biggest and the brightest—you could see some color too, kind of pink. Next, was the Moon, which was a small crescent. In the middle were Venus and Mars, kind of close together. On the bottom of the string was Saturn, then Mercury. We took turns looking at them. Mars really was red, and Saturn had a big ring around it—neat. Mr. Horn slipped his camera on the lens and snapped a bunch of pictures. We all took turns again, marveling at the idea that you could actually see something that far away—millions of light years—and that's far.

Victoria wanted to share her moment, and called home after her last turn. "Oh, Mother," she exclaimed, "It's beautiful. It's the neatest thing I've ever seen. I had to call and tell you." Then she was quiet for a moment. "I'm sorry I scared you. No, nothing is wrong. I was just so enthralled. You can see for yourself after we get the pictures."

Mr. Horn broke in. "Tell them we'll be ready to leave here in about fifteen minutes—home in one hour." Victoria relayed the message. It was a good idea; Victoria gave him thumbs up.

Victoria took a deep breath, and started rolling up the hose. "Boy, sometimes parents can be a pain."

Mr. Horn was right, and we pulled out in exactly fifteen minutes. Victoria and I just sat there on the back seat. I guess we were thinking about how neat it was to see part of our universe—how we could actually see millions of miles with our eyes. I slipped for a moment and my hand touched hers. She didn't pull away; she just looked at me and smiled. I smiled back. In a couple of minutes, we hit a bump that caused me to lift up my hand. I was afraid to put it back. Victoria kept looking at me, though, and I kind of liked that—she had a neat smile.

———————————

Mr. Horn got his pictures back in a couple of days. He made a CD for both of us, and loaned us his projector to use during the presentation. Boy, the pictures filled the whole screen in the science classroom—the kids were going to love them. Victoria's chart was really good, too, and made it easier for me to explain how you they were all going to line up again in 2040.

Finally, the big day came. At breakfast, Mom decided I didn't have the right clothes on and made me change twice. She also plastered down my hair with some kind of smelly stuff—how embarrasing if someone noticed. When I got to the classroom I checked the list and found out we got to go first. That was good because most of the class really paid attention early on. I was right the kids loved the pictures. So did Mrs. Williams—getting an A was going to be a shoo in.

When everyone was finished, we got to go to the cafeteria early. I sat down with Victoria. It was okay to sit with a girl after a special deal like a presentation. Anyway, she was real happy, and talked about every little thing we did—over and over. I was happy with the presentation too, but not that happy.

Then she said Jack had told her about me going to Laredo. Now that did surprise me. Why would Jack want to tell her that? Maybe it was because he was going to visit me for the summer—kind of bragging. "I've already been to Laredo," Victoria said out of the blue.

I almost fell over. "You've been to Laredo?"

"Yes. When I visited my aunt last summer. Her name is Virginia Porter. She lives in Houston and is the head of the language department at Rice—that's a university there. Anyway, part of the year she runs a language school for Border Patrol students in Laredo. I went with her on one of her visits—she helps teach. We only stayed down there for about two weeks. The school is right there at the airport."

"Is it awful? I asked, almost afraid to hear the answer.

She thought for a minute. "Not real awful," she said carefully. "I mean there wasn't anything for me to do. There weren't any kids there my age. You know how that can be, hanging out with adults all the time. All I did was read and study."

I nodded in agreement. I'd been there. "Yeah. That can be a bummer. Dad says it's hot all the time—is it?"

"Yep. It was real hot when I was there. It gets to be over a hundred every day. But it's okay in the air conditioning," she added smiling, after seeing the shock on my face.

"I don't think it's going to be much fun there," I said, feeling kind of bad after thinking about all that hot weather. I'd been right all along it was almost a wasteland.

Victoria leaned closer. "You can have fun anywhere if you want to," she said. "It's all in the way you <u>look</u> at things." She was probably repeating what her aunt told her.

I replied quickly. "Well I <u>look</u> at Laredo as <u>hot</u>."

She persisted with her logic. "It's hot here too, and the humidity is much higher. That's what makes you feel like it's hotter than it really is."

Maybe she had something there, but I still wasn't convinced. "I don't know. It's almost like another country—almost like Mexico."

She perked up. "I can teach you some Spanish. It's not too hard—if you want to learn," she added, after seeing my surprise. She kept at it. "Listen to this: *Hola, Amigo. Como esta usted? Estoy bien, gracias.* Could you understand any of that?"

"Are you kidding? No!"

"I said, hello, friend. How are you? The friend replies: I am fine, thank you. See, it's easy." My face must have been red. "Don't be embarrassed, you can do it."

That made it worse. "I'm not embarrassed, I just don't want to." She just looked at me. Of course, I just knew I was red, now.

Jack walked up. "Hi, you guys. Your science thing was good. I really liked the pictures of the planets." He did a double take. "Eddie! Why are you so red?"

"He's too embarrassed to try speaking Spanish," Victoria chipped in before I could answer.

Oh. No. That would be just the opening Jack was looking for. I saw his eyes light up. "Are you <u>afraid</u> you can't do it, Jack?" He had a huge grin on his face.

Victoria gave him a glare. "Of course he's not afraid. He's just apprehensive." She gave me kind of an I'm-sorry-look, and then rattled off a bunch of Spanish to Jack. It caught him by surprise and caused his big smile to disappear. "See," she said. "It's just confusing the first time you hear it." Jack knew better than to argue with her—and he knew when he was beat. He quickly turned to leave. When he was behind her, he stuck out his tongue and put his thumbs in his ears—wiggling his fingers. "I know you're back there, stupid," she said without looking. Jack ran for it. "Okay, Eddie. *Hola amigo. Como esta usted.* Come on—say it."

Man, she was persistent. "Okay, but just once." *Hold it amigo, Como staaa ousted.*

A huge smile erupted over her face. "Good. Let's try it again."

She kept at it until I had it down pretty good. When I walked in the door after school, I whipped it on Mom. *Hola, amiga. Como esta usted.*

She about fainted. "Wow! That's terrific. How nice of Victoria to help you." How did she know it was Victoria? How'd she always know that stuff? "Here, I made some cookies," she continued, "Sit down and tell me how your presentation went." I'd do most anything for a nice warm chocolate chip cookie, so I sat down, and filled her in.

Mom seemed real happy and calm, so I decided to ask her a couple of things. "Mom. When am I going to get bigger? I mean, Dad's pretty tall. I hope I'm not going to be short my whole life."

Her eyes lit up big time, and she took my hand. Ah oh. I should have known better than to ask her then, after talking about Victoria and all. "Don't worry, Eddie. Boys grow in spurts. You will probably grow six inches in the next few months." She nodded her encouragement, then added, "You were a long baby, twenty-two inches, so you should be at least as big as Jim. He's six foot two."

I reached for another cookie and stood up. "Thanks, Mom. I was getting kind of worried. I mean Jack's so short, I don't want to be little like him."

She shook her head. "Jack's not short, and he's going to spurt up too, wait, and see. Caroline told me he was a long baby too."

"He'll be glad to hear that, I said, grabbing another cookie. "Guess I'd better walk Andy now."

She smiled, and picked up the cookies. "Remember, Eddie. You can always talk to me about anything that's bothering you."

"Sure, Mom," I said, turning to leave, knowing that I would probably get one of those silly winks from Mom when I mentioned Victoria again.

———————————

Things went pretty good for the next couple of weeks. I got A in science and math, and a B in everything else. Mom and Dad were happy with my grades. Victoria kept pestering me to learn Spanish, and I did manage to learn a few more things—although I fought about it with her tooth and nail. I couldn't let her think I liked it—could I.

About the end of May, Dad called home and said we would be flying to Laredo with him—on the Gulfstream—and Jack could go with us. He had to pick up some parts, or something, and got permission from the CI....oops, from the Government Agency he worked for. He also told us he had found a house for us. He said it was a little old, but it had a new air conditioning system and was nice and clean. Mom liked the last part best.

Of course, Jack was ecstatic. Me too, I had been wondering if I could make due on my promise that we would have a flying adventure. Whew! I secretly hoped that some other good stuff would happen right away, so he wouldn't be so down in the dumps all the time. The only down side of the deal was that I had to help get everything packed up—at both Jack's apartment and my house too. Oh. Well.

Before we knew it, the moving truck picked up our stuff and headed west—or was it north. Then I remembered. He had to go north before he could go west—there was only water to the west.

The day before we were going to leave, Mrs. Thomas called and told Mom that Victoria was going to visit her aunt in Houston this summer, and thought she might visit Laredo. Mom said that was wonderful news, and told her that Jack and I would be happy to keep her company while she was there. I wasn't sure how Victoria would fit in helping Jack and I wash airplanes, but it might be kind of fun having her there. Maybe she could translate for us—that would be something useful, at least.

I decided not to worry about it now, there were a million other things to do. Jack stayed over the last night so he could get used to not being with his mom. Is that dumb or what? Anyway, our adventure was about to begin.

CHAPTER FIVE

The next morning Jack's mom drove us to Homestead Air Force Base, where Dad would be. We had a million suitcases and a couple of boxes—plus Andy's dog crate. Boy, I hope that plane is big enough for everything. If not I guess we could leave the dog crate, Andy didn't like it anyway.

When we got to the flight line, we saw Dad taxi to his parking spot. The Gulfstream was a pretty big airplane—Dad called it an intermediate corporate jet. Anyway, it looked sleek and fast. The plane was all white, and had two engines mounted back toward the tail. There were all kinds of things, called antennas, sticking out of the top and bottom of the plane. They were for spotting other airplanes and listening to pilots and the people they were talking to on their radios. That's why he was in Laredo, to spot other airplanes that were trying to smuggle illegal stuff into the United States—neat huh?

Wow! The airplane was bigger than it looked when we started out to get on board. It must have been fifty feet long, and the wings were big too—almost as long, maybe longer than the body, I guessed. There was a truck there pumping fuel when we arrived, so we had to return to the holding area to wait until they finished. Jack was really impressed. I could tell, his mouth was open for the whole time.

A little later Dad signaled to us that it was time to board. As we were leaving the holding area, Jack's mom gave him a hug and broke into tears. That was all Jack needed, and he puckered up a bit too. I looked away, pretending I hadn't seen him cry.

After we finished handing all the stuff to Dad, including Andy, we climbed up a collapsible ladder built onto the door. The plane was full of electronic stuff. Mom and Andy got to sit near the back where there were regular seats, but Dad sat Jack and I at one of the consoles. He gave us headsets to put on so we could hear all of the radio talk—cool. I had to admit I was a bit apprehensive; after all, I hadn't flown since I was six.

In a minute or two, we heard voices one of them was Dad. "Ready to start engines, chief."

"All clear." The crew chief said.

"Starting number two," Dad said. "Starter engaged. Ten, twenty percent. Engine master, on. I've got ignition, throttle idle. Generators on line, bus tie closed. All instruments, green. Ready to start number one." He repeated the process on the other engine. I don't know why he did them backwards, maybe it was because the number two engine was on the other side from the door, in case there was a problem.

"This is neat," Jack said, giving me a thumbs up.

Dad continued. "Homestead tower. Gulfstream nine zero one ready to taxi." He gave some kind of a signal to the crew chief who then pulled the blocks from in front of the wheels.

"Roger, nine zero one. Taxi runway two nine zero. Altimeter two niner, niner two."

"Roger, two niner, niner two." The engines speeded up and we started to move. Jack looked at me with a big grin on his face. We headed out toward the main runway and stopped at the end. "Homestead, nine zero one is number one, ready for takeoff."

"Roger, nine zero one. Winds are two seven zero at fourteen knots, cleared for takeoff."

"Roger, tower." Dad pulled in the middle of the runway and stopped. The engines revved up until the whole airplane was shaking. Then it suddenly leaped forward, causing me to be pushed backwards. "Nine zero one is rolling."

I could hear Dad's co-pilot talking to him. "Eighty knots, all instruments green. One twenty, V-one. Looks good, V-two, let's fly." Then dad pulled back on the wheel, the nose lifted off, and suddenly we were airborne. I looked over at Jack and he had the biggest smile on his face I had ever seen.

Then the co-pilot said. "Gear." We could hear a noise and a thump. "Gear up and locked. Flaps." There was a whirring noise and the airplane kind of sank for a minute. "Flaps up," the co-pilot continued. "Instruments green—feed tank full," takeoff checklist complete."

"Roger," Dad said. "Homestead, nine zero one requests clearance to departure control."

"Roger, nine zero one, cleared three two two point five. Have a good trip."

"Thanks, tower."

"Frequency set," Dad's co-pilot said.

"Miami departure, Gulfstream nine zero one, glades departure three, passing ten thousand."

"Roger, nine zero one. We have your beacon. Cleared present position direct Control twelve twenty-six, flight plan route. Have a good day. Contact

Tallahassee Center on three two eight point two. Good day."

"Roger, Miami. Thanks.

"Frequency set," the copilot said.

"Tallahassee Center, Gulfstream nine zero one, passing flight level two one zero, requesting four five zero."

"Roger, nine zero one. I have your beacon. Cleared Flight Level four five zero. Sky conditions reported clear, no turbulence. Contact Houston Center abeam New Orleans on three three one point six. Have a good flight, good-day."

"I copy. Thanks Jacksonville."

Boy, things happened fast when you were flying. Then Dad's copilot, Leo Jacobs suddenly appeared. "You guys want to fly for a while?"

Jack's eyes perked up when he heard. He looked at me. I nodded and gave him a thumbs up. We released our safety harnesses and walked forward to the flight deck. Dad was sitting in the left seat. He motioned for Jack to sit down in the right seat. I stood right beside him in the middle. I could tell that Jack was a little nervous.

After he settled down, Dad flipped off the autopilot and told Jack to take the wheel. Jack cautiously eased his hands on the wheel and the airplane bounced a little bit. Then Dad showed him how to make a little turn. Jack did pretty well; at least he didn't turn upside down or anything.

After a couple of turns, Dad took control. "Jack. Look out the windshield. Do you see the horizon?" Jack nodded. "Well, this instrument," he pointed to a pretty big instrument in the middle of a million dials, "is called an artificial horizon." It was kind of like a circle, painted light blue on the top and black on the bottom. There was also a little airplane in the middle, like you were seeing it from the back.

Dad continued, "See the line in the middle? The blue part is the sky above the horizon, and the black part is the sky below the horizon. What you want to do is keep the little airplane right on that line— which is level flight. That's how you fly in the clouds."

Dad gave the controls back to Jack. "Wow," Jack kept saying—over and over. He also had a smile on that seemed taped to his face. He was doing pretty good until he got a little cocky and turned to quick. The airplane bounced quite a bit and started down. Jack's smile turned to terror and he threw up his hands—eyes all bugged out.

"I've got it, Jack," Dad said, as he took the controls. "You've done very well. But let that be a lesson for you—you always have to pay close attention to your attitude. Things can get out of hand pretty quick." Then Dad let him fly again. Jack paid a lot more attention this time. In a few minutes, his knuckles started getting white from gripping the wheel so tight. Dad noticed right away and had him change places with me.

"Okay, Eddie, show me what you can do." I tried my best to be smooth and paid a lot of attention to the artificial horizon, but I did the same thing Jack did eventually. It was harder than it looked, so I didn't feel too bad for making a couple of mistakes—since Jack did too.

After a while, Dad took the controls and pointed out where New Orleans should be. It was real hazy up there over the Gulf of Mexico— neither Jack nor I could see the city, just the muddy water where the Mississippi River empties into the Gulf. All you could see was miles and miles of water on all sides. I hoped Dad knew where we were going. It was kind of unnerving up there in the sky all by yourself, with nothing but water below. Then Dad told us to look straight up. Wow, the sky was almost black when you looked straight up. Dad said it was because the we were not too far from the edge of the atmosphere at forty-five thousand feet—almost ten miles up. About then, Leo showed up and Dad told us to return to our seats.

Jack and I kind of wrestled around for a while after leaving the flight deck. I guess it was because we were so excited—or because flying gave us some kind of charge or something. Boy, it was really fun, though—and kind of scary at the same time. No wonder Dad like flying so much.

We went back and were telling Mom about our flying experiences when we started to descend. Dad called us on the airplane speaker and said to look out the right windows—that we were passing Houston. "That's Galveston Bay in front of Houston. The city of Galveston is on the end of that long island at the entrance to the Bay." It was real clear and we could see the whole area. "We'll be turning left in a minute. You can see the Padre barrier islands running down the coast all the way to Mexico. The city on that Bay to the left is Corpus Christi. We'll be turning slightly right there and Laredo will be right on our nose, a little over one hundred and twenty miles away. We'll be on the ground in less than thirty minutes. Better buckle up, boys."

We scurried for our seats and put on our belts and headsets—just in time to hear Dad on the radio. "Houston Center, nine zero one requesting flight level two four zero."

"Roger nine zero one. Cleared to Flight Level two zero zero. Laredo altimeter three zero one seven. Weather is clear. Squawk Mode three C. Contact Laredo approach departing Flight Level two four zero. Good-day."

"Copy, Houston. Thanks." "Boys," Dad said. "If your ears feel funny, hold your nose and blow. That will clear them." Both of us tried to see what would happen—our ears popped—cool.

"Laredo approach, nine zero one leaving two four zero. Requesting a VFR landing."

"Roger, nine zero one. Cleared present position direct Laredo. Cleared to Laredo tower, three one three point one.

"Roger thanks."

"Laredo. Gulfstream nine zero one. Request landing instructions.

"Roger, nine zero one, welcome home. Cleared VFR approach runway one eight zero left. Altimeter three zero one six. Winds out of the south at seven knots. We have a Cessna one seventy-two on final for a full stop on one eight zero right. Call two miles."

"Roger, Laredo. We're on an extended base at six miles." There was a little delay. Then the gear went down with a thump. "Laredo, nine zero one, two miles."

"Nine zero one. Cleared to land, your traffic has cleared the runway."

"Thanks, Laredo. Gear down and locked."

We heard a whirring noise and saw the wing flaps go down. Then the co-pilot started reading off the airspeed. Before I knew it, there was the ground and I heard a squeak almost at the same time—we had landed. "Welcome to Laredo, guys," Dad said over the mike as we turned off the runway.

Jack and I looked at each other, both smiling. We gave each other a thumbs up. Our adventure had really started.

CHAPTER SIX

There was a lot of commotion when we got off the airplane. Jack and I wanted to look all over the outside of the Gulfstream, and Mom wanted us to get the luggage. Guess who won? Dad had to do some paperwork or something, but came back pretty soon with a van. He helped us load everything in the back. Of course, Mom had to hold Andy, while we did all the work. It didn't take too long, though, till we left for our new house.

Jack and I were jumping around in back; trying to see the other planes and stuff, but Dad just whisked us straight off of the airport. He hardly even slowed down when we passed the Lone Star Flying Service, the place he told us we could work. "Sit down and behave, you guys, and keep your belts on. You'll have plenty of time to see everything out here," he said, forcefully. "As a matter of fact, before the week is over,

I'll bet you'll be griping your heads off because you have nothing to do." Mom was nodding her head, so I guess she agreed with Dad—as usual.

It was only a little way to our new house. Actually, it wasn't new; it looked old when we pulled into the driveway. There wasn't even a garage, only a carport—and hardly any yard. Well, I guess that would make mowing easier, I thought, remembering what Victoria told me about thinking positive.

Anyway, it wasn't so bad inside, at least in the front part; there just wasn't hardly any furniture. Then I noticed that there weren't any rugs either—all the floors were big old reddish-brown tile. Andy took off a mile a minute after I let him out of his cage. He smelled everything in the place, and then started over. "Where's our room, Mom?" I yelled as I started searching the rest of the house.

"The one with the bunk beds," Dad yelled back, carrying suitcases into their room.

"Come on, Jack. It's this room, the one at the very back corner. Keen, there's a bathroom right next door." Andy found me and immediately jumped up on the lower bunk, made a nest, curled up, and went to sleep—guess he'd had a hard day flying and all.

Jack came running in and instantly claimed the top bunk. "Dibs on the top," he yelled, swinging himself up over the end. He sat there on the mattress and kind of bounced up and down, daring me to drag him off. I thought about it for a minute, and then realized that I didn't really want the top bunk. Besides, Andy couldn't get up there.

I decided I had to challenge him for it, though. "Maybe we ought to flip for it. I reached in my pocket and pulled out the nickel I had stashed there. "What do you want, heads, or tails?"

"I don't want either. I got here first, and I'm your guest—remember? You should give me first choice."

I tried to look kind of beaten. "Well, okay. I guess I have to. But that's the last free one, everything else we have to flip for, okay? He grinned like a fool, stuck his tongue out, and wagged his head back and forth. Boy, I just know he can't be twelve.

"Eddie. You and Jack come get your stuff," Mom hollered from the living room.

"Okay, Mom. Come on, Jack. I'm not carrying your junk." Jack jumped off the bed and almost knocked me over. "Watch it, dummy, you could have killed me." I slugged him.

"I didn't mean it. You'd be dead if I did."

"Oh. Yeah!"

"Eddie!"

"Coming, Mom. See, you're going to get me in trouble. Let's get our stuff and then look around outside." We hit the door at the same time and I got squished. "Ouch! Grow up, Jack."

"Hi, Mrs. Matthews the room is neat," Jack said, sucking up to Mom. "Where do you want me to put my stuff?"

"I'm glad you like it, Jack. There are six drawers built into one side of the closet. Just open the doors, you'll see them. Both you and Eddie can share—three drawers each."

"Yes, Mrs. Matthews." Jack picked up his suitcase and tried to trip me when I reached for mine.

"Ha. Missed me." I grabbed my big old canvas bag and headed for our room, trying to beat Jack to the door. It was close, but I won. I opened the closet and found the drawers. "I'll take the top three."

"Oh, no you don't. You said we were going to flip for it."

Man, this was going to be a hassle, flipping for everything. I flipped my nickel and held my hand over it. "Heads or Tails?" Jack thought for a minute, trying to decide. "Hurry up, nitwit. Don't you ever want to go outside?"

"Heads."

"It's Tails. I'll take the top three drawers. You get the bottom, shorty. Ha. Ha."

"I'm only about an inch shorter than you," he fumed.

"No you're not. You're two inches shorter."

"Not any more. I grew."

He was starting to get mad. He hates it that he's littler than me. "Okay, one inch. But that's only until we officially get measured again."

I started putting my things in the dresser the way Mom insisted: All the socks together in the top drawer—rolled up, along with my underwear—kind of folded. In the second drawer would go all of my tee shirts and sweaters. The third drawer held my folded up pants and outside shorts and stuff like that. Then I noticed, Jack. "Hey, Mom will have a cat-fit if you just dump everything in the drawers all mixed up."

"Why? I can find everything okay."

I knew I had to work on him about this. "Well Mom generally puts things away for you after she washes. If you don't do it right, you'll have to get everything out of the laundry room and put it away yourself." That kind of got his attention, I could tell he didn't want to go get stuff all the time.

"How do I have to fix it?" I showed him the way she liked it. Boy, his mom must have been easy, he didn't know how to do anything.

Finally, we were finished. Mom started making our beds when we left for the backyard. Boy, I thought, I'm going to have to teach Jack how to make the bed too. What a hassle this summer is going to be.

Just as we were about to go out to the backyard, Mom called. "Eddie. Are you going out back?"

"Yes, Mom."

"Would you please check every bit of the fence for holes. I don't want Andy to get out if we leave him in the backyard. He doesn't know his way around here and he could get lost. I'm going to get him a new nametag with our address on it, and a new rabies-tag as well—but until I get them, we have to be extra careful. I don't want him outside without a leash, and only in the backyard if we know he can't get out, understand?"

"Sure, Mom. We'll check the fence right now. Come on, Jack, this is important. Andy, come on, big boy. Come show us if you can find any holes in the fence." Andy came running out of our bedroom, eager to cooperate. "Don't let him get too far away, Jack, in case he finds a hole."

"Don't you want to put him on his leash?"

"Na, he wouldn't look for holes with his leash on—he's got to be loose."

"Okay, but don't blame me if he gets out. I don't want your mom mad at me for doing something you did."

Andy found three holes right away. "See, worry-wart, he wouldn't have found them with his leash on."

"You're just lucky. It's a wonder he isn't a mile down the street chasing a cat or something."

"What do you know, you don't have a dog." Just then, Andy let out a yelp and ran like crazy to the back of the carport. We followed him and caught him digging like everything in a good-sized hole that went down under the house. "What is it Andy?"

Hearing the commotion, Dad came out. "What's going on?"

"Andy found something down that hole." Andy looked up, wagging his tail like crazy—all proud of himself.

"Oh. I forgot to tell you, an Armadillo lives there. He won't hurt anything, and Andy will never catch him—he's too smart for a city-born schnauzer."

Jack looked at me kind of worried. "What's an Armadillo? Do they bite?"

"No," Dad said. "Not if you don't try and pick him up—but if you do, watch out. Come on, Mom made some sandwiches. Aren't you hungry?" Andy was, he followed Dad inside.

Jack gave one last look at the hole. I think he was kind of scared. I reminded myself to show him a picture of one in my nature book when our stuff arrived. "Don't worry, Jack, they usually don't come out until night."

"Glad I got the top bunk," Jack said as we walked in the kitchen. Boy, he was scared.

"Hey, Dad. We need some wire screen to fix three holes in the fence. By the way, what do Armadillo's eat? Do we have to feed it?"

"The landlord said to roll a couple of raw eggs down his hole every couple of days. He said that would keep him from bothering us. They eat bugs most of the time, which helps keep them out of the house. Kind of an organic pest control service." He grinned, proud of his joke.

Mom didn't think it was so funny. "If I see one roach, you are going to hire a professional," she said, which quickly wiped that silly grin off his face. "All I've got is peanut butter and jelly—and milk and coffee. That will have to hold you until I can do some real shopping—and when our stuff gets here. I can't cook without pots and pans."

"We can always get pizza," Jack spoke up. "I like pizza."

I frowned at him, knowing Mom wasn't crazy about pizza. "I don't know if they even make pizza here. We're almost in Mexico. Mom, what do they eat here?"

"The same stuff we ate in Homestead," Dad piped in. "But that gives me an idea. Let's go out for Mexican food tonight, honey? I know a great little restaurant—it's family style, and will give the boys a chance to try everything."

"Mom's eyes lit up. Great idea. I am a little tired, and I could sure use a Margarita. Thanks, sweetheart." She gave him a quick kiss. I decided not to protest, she seemed so happy.

"Eddie, I'm going to stop by Home Depot after lunch to get some wire. I want you to show me the damaged areas first, so I'll know what and how much to get. Then I'll help you fix them. Are you sure, there are just three holes?

I thought for a minute. "Well, there might be a couple of other places that aren't quite holes yet." I said, just in case Andy had missed something.

"Okay. I'll get enough for a few extra holes." He winked at Mom. Boy, they sure liked to wink at each other a lot, along with all that hugging and kissing. Parents are strange.

"Eddie! Don't wipe your hands on your shirt. I don't have my washer yet, and I don't want you running around with jelly on your shirt. That goes for you too, Jack." He had peanut butter all over his chin and Mom handed him a napkin.

"Yes, Mrs. Matthews," he blurted out. "I'll watch it from now on." That brought out another one of those dumb winks from Dad.

———————————

Jack and I just hung around the house for the rest of the day, kind of getting to know the lay of the land. I did find another hole in the fence, so I kept Andy in the house. He didn't care, he wanted to take a nap. After all, he sleeps all day when I'm gone to school. The back yard was actually bigger than it looked, so I told Jack that he would have to help me mow it. He didn't seem to mind so much, except I think he figured I was going to pay him for it. Boy, will he be surprised.

Mom had us help with a few things around the house. We had to break down cardboard boxes and put the suitcases in the attic, but it wasn't too bad. Then, we had to help Dad fix the holes in the fence. Wouldn't you know it, he found three more holes. They weren't actually holes—just kind of bare spots. I told him they weren't big enough for Andy, but he fixed them anyway. Dads are like that, they go nuts once they start fixing something.

Then Jack and I went in, sat on our beds, and talked for a while. Mainly about our flying experiences and stuff. Then we quieted down, so I decided to do a little planning. We both saw some pretty neat stuff at the airport when we drove home, and were anxious to check it out. I thought that maybe we could go tomorrow, if the mover didn't come. Hmmm. Maybe I ought to figure when he will get here. Let's see, he left on a Saturday and said he was going to drive straight through. I guess he couldn't just drive right here without sleeping, so I would have to allow a couple of nights for that—maybe three. Hmmm. Fifty miles per hour for twelve hours a day—that's six hundred miles. Wait, I had to take off for eating and gassing up. I decided to make it five hundred miles. Dad said it was around two thousand miles total. That's easy, it would take four days. "Oh. Nuts. Four days is tomorrow," I blurted out, waking up Jack.

"Huh? What's going on? Is it time to eat?"

"No, Jack. I just figured that the mover is going to come tomorrow. That means we can't go to the base—we'll have to help here."

"Why do I have to help? It's not my stuff."

"Just because you do. Quit griping, it won't be a lot of work. You know, just helping kind of work. Besides, the quicker Mom gets her cooking stuff, the quicker you can eat good."

Jack moaned a little, but didn't actually complain. He was smarter than that—he liked Mom's cooking.

———————————————

About five o'clock, Mom called us. "Eddie. Jack. I want you two to take a shower and put on some clean clothes. We'll be going to dinner as soon as your dad gets back from work.

"But, Mom. We aren't even dirty," I protest for the both of us.

"Yes you are. You just don't know it. Besides, you need to try out the shower."

I decided she wasn't going to give up. "Okay, Mom. You go first, Jack."

"Oh. No you don't. I'm not going to try out the shower for you. If it doesn't work good you'll blame me."

"No I wouldn't. I was just thinking you were the guest and I was going to give you firsts."

"Let's flip," he said jumping down from the top bunk. "I'm feeling lucky."

He was grinning like a nut—as usual. "Okay." I got my nickel. Man, it was getting a workout today.

"Tails," Jack called before I flipped. I put it tails up and flipped. Someone said it always comes out opposite when you do that. "Ha. It's tails. I win. You shower first," he piled on the bunk and laid there giggling.

I tried the shower. Actually, it worked pretty good, except the water was getting a little cold by the time I finished. "Okay, Jack. Hurry up, it works fine." I tossed my dirty clothes on the floor and put on clean stuff. I did seem to smell a little better. Maybe rolling around on the ground fixing that wire got me dirtier than I though.

"Yow!" I heard from the shower. Jack was screaming. "You bum! You used all the hot water." I played like I didn't hear him. He'd know for sure if he saw me, and know I'd set him up, cause I was all red-faced from laughing.

"I get first next time, Eddie. I'll fix you. I want to see how you like taking a shower in ice water," he fumed.

I tried to act surprised. "Huh? What are you talking about?"

He tossed his dirty clothes on top of mine and hurriedly dressed. I decided to carry all the stuff out to the laundry room, just this once—he was mad enough.

We walked into the kitchen and Mom took a look at us. "I want you boys to go back to the bathroom and comb your hair—and brush your teeth while you're at it. You need to brush after you eat, and you missed after lunch—didn't you?" We nodded and retreated to the bathroom.

"Boy," Jack said, "All moms are the same. They never miss nothin." I nodded, reaching for my toothbrush.

———————————

Dad got home just as we finished. "You guys look pretty spiffy," he said, kissing Mom. "Good news, the movers are coming tomorrow. Be here about ten." I knew it, I thought, wishing I had brought it up earlier—now Dad got all the credit.

"Terrific," Mom answered, "Are you going to be able to help?"

"I have to go in for a while in the morning, but I'll be here no later than noon."

"That's good. But I have two big strong helpers here—don't I?" She stood between us and held our shoulders. Both of us must have had a sour look on our faces, because Dad gave us that knock-it-off look.

I chimed in quickly. "We don't mind helping you, Mom. We're big enough for <u>most</u> of the stuff—if it's not <u>too</u> heavy." I added, hoping that she would re-think her decision. Nuts, she didn't pick up on that one, or she just ignored me—Mom is good at that. She just headed for the bathroom to freshen up, whatever that was. Oh well, you can't win them all.

Dad came back from their bedroom. He had also changed into clean stuff. I'll bet he brushed his teeth too, I thought. Mom had everybody trained in our house.

In a couple of minutes, Mom was back, smelling good. Maybe that's what she means by freshening up. We piled in the car and Dad turned toward downtown. He stopped at a dumpy looking place. "Well, this is it."

I looked at Jack. He was wearing his worried look. Mom didn't seem to mind, though. She trusted, Dad.

We went inside. It was kind of dark and pretty cool. There were all kinds of Mexican things around: pots, cactus, pictures, things like that. It smelled pretty good, though, so I guess it wouldn't be too bad. A waitress came over to greet us. *"Como esta. Bienvenido."*

Without thinking, I answered her. *"Estoy bien, gracias."* Everyone looked at me kind of funny. Kind of like they didn't know, I could speak a little Spanish. Boy, Victoria would have been proud of me. The waitress put her hand on my shoulder. *"Bueno. Maravilloso. Si Hablo Espanol."*

"Solo un poco," I answered her, my face turning red.

"That's good. But I think you will learn to speak more than a little, she said, leading our group to a big table near the back. "Now," she said, after everyone was seated, "What would you like to eat?"

Dad spoke up. I think we'd like your family dinner. The boys, here, would like to try everything.

"Bien." She said, smiling. "The bus-boy will bring you some salsa and tortilla chips right away. Water for everyone?"

Dad shook his head. "I'll have a beer…*cerveza, por favor.* How about you, *senhora*?"

Mom followed his lead. "I want a big *Margarita, senhor. Agua* will be fine for the *muchachos*." The waitress nodded and jotted it down on her pad, smiling as she left.

Oh, man, now they are going to embarrass me for the rest of the night. Just because I was trying to be polite. Jack just sat there. I guess he didn't know how to act international.

We started by dipping the chips into the salsa. It was a little hot, but we liked it. Next, the waitress brought a couple of big platters of stuff called, tamales, and enchiladas. They were a little spicy too, but really good. There were also bowls of tangy rice and two kinds of beans, one kind was all mashed up. We made little rolled up sandwiches out of the beans, using some flat things called, soft tacos, or tortillas, whatever—they were good, but messy. There was also a salad of gunky green stuff called, guacamole, it was okay, kind of tasted like avocados, though—not my favorite. We sprinkled grated cheese over everything. The only thing that Jack and I didn't each much of was the jalapeno peppers. I took a big bite out of one and my mouth just about exploded—it was <u>real</u> hot. Jack wouldn't even try his, the chicken. We were too full when it came time for dessert. Jack and I were stuffed. Mom had some pudding looking stuff called flan. It didn't look too bad, so Jack and I decided to try it next time.

I said *Buenas Noches* to our waitress when we left, wanting to be polite and everything. We piled in the car and headed for home. Suddenly, I was really tired. After thinking about it, we'd had a pretty neat day—long though. I wondered what tomorrow would bring. Maybe living in Laredo wouldn't be so bad after all.

Jack and I jumped onto our beds as soon as we got home, even though it was only eight thirty. Andy, joined me and fixed his pillow at the foot of the bed. *"Buenas Noches,"* I said.

The next morning was pretty normal. I had to teach Jack a few more things about our household routine, you know, things that would keep him out of trouble with Mom and Dad. He was scared of Dad, by the way, not having one around his place. Dad was kind of loud sometimes when he wanted you to do something, and he made Jack jump. I told him not to worry, that he would get used to all his hollering, that he really wasn't the one to worry about—it was Mom. Jack picked up on all of my lessons real quick. He could be smart when he wanted to be.

The movers showed up early, eight o'clock. The driver was the same guy from Florida, but he had a whole new group of helpers. This time they were all Mexicans—or Hispanics—I wasn't sure which name I was supposed to use. The boss had Mom stand in the living room and tell the workers where to take everything. They were better than the guys in Florida, because they didn't gripe and rest all of the time. They were also a lot more careful and didn't bump into walls and stuff like the others.

Anyway, Jack and I didn't have to do much. We only carried junk for Mom, and kept Andy out of the way. Piece of cake—for a while.

Then Dad came home. He started ordering us around and had us putting away everything in sight. At last, Mom saved us. "Jim, don't be in such a hurry. I want to take my time and put things away where I want them. I don't want to have to re-do it later." Dad nodded.

I looked at Jack. "See, I told you Mom ran everything." He understood completely.

About that time, the movers had everything off the truck and most of the stuff unpacked.

There were glasses and vases and all kinds of things sitting on every table and counter in the house. Mom started washing most of it while Dad put shelf paper in the cabinets. Suddenly I realized what was about to happen, and I tried to get Jack out of there before Mom discovered she needed dryers for the stuff she was washing. "Eddie, Jack, I need some help."

Nuts! Too late, she caught us. Both Jack and I dried for hours. Finally, my stomach started yelling for food. "Mom. How about if Jack and I make us all peanut butter sandwiches? I'm hungry, aren't you?"

Mom checked her watch. "Oh, my. It's already past one. That would be nice, Eddie. Make a couple for Dad too."

"Yes, Mom. Come on, Jack, let's fix us something to eat." We made a ton of sandwiches. "Mom, we're out of jelly," I said, admiring the giant stack of sandwiches we made. Jack couldn't stand it, he'd already started on his.

Mom came over to the table. Her eyes bugged out. "Wow. That's a lot of sandwiches."

She yelled at Dad, who was in the bedroom working. "Come on, Jim, lunch. I hope you're hungry."

That afternoon Mom went to the store and picked up a bunch of groceries. Oh. Boy, she was going to make us fried chicken. Pretty soon, the house was full of good smells—just like home. Actually, I guess it was home.

We ate way too much at dinner. Mmmm. Mom sure could cook I think she noticed how much Jack liked her stuff too. He was happy as a hog at her dinner table. He did screw up saying Grace, but I told him not to worry, he'd get the hang of it pretty soon.

We got out of drying the dishes because Jack had to call his mom and tell her that everything was fine. Mom also talked with Mrs. Davis for a little bit to make sure she wasn't too worried about Jack. Moms are like that, you know.

Dad told us at dinner that we could go to the airport with him the next morning that he would leave us in the care of Cody Corbett, the owner of Lone Star Flying Service. That sounded pretty good to Jack and I, so after we took out the trash, we went to our bedroom to plan out the next day—even though we didn't know what to expect. We decided to go to sleep early, so we'd be good and ready for some adventure. Andy joined us while we talked in the dark, trying to decide what had been the most fun so far. We settled on the airplane ride and the Armadillo.

We had to get up early because Dad left at seven-thirty, so we finally gave up about nine-thirty, after talking for an hour. I think Jack felt happier now, at least he wasn't moping around and slugging me all the time. I felt pretty good, too. I just laid there in the dark, relaxing for a while before I went to sleep. My mind was still going a mile a minute, thinking about what was going to happen tomorrow. "You asleep yet, Eddie?" Jack whispered.

"No. I was thinking about tomorrow."

"Me too. Think we'll have fun?"

"Sure, why not? Haven't you had fun so far?"

Jack hesitated for a minute. "You know, I don't think I ever had so much fun."

"Well, it won't be much fun at six in the morning if we don't get any sleep."

"Okay. *Bonis nochus*, Eddie," Jack said, trying to impress me.

"It's *Buenas Nochus, Juan,* that's your name in Spanish in case you're wondering."

"*Juan*, that's neat." He repeated it for a million times, over and over.

"Knock it off, *Juan*, I'm tired."

With that, we quieted down. I think Andy was glad. He let out a groan and took a deep breath. Buenas Noches, Andy, I thought.

CHAPTER SEVEN

"Psssst. Eddie. Time to get up," Dad said, quietly, giving me a little shake on the shoulder. Andy groaned and smushed down on his pillow.

"What time is it, Dad?" I mumbled, yawning.

He whispered, "About six-thirty. You guys had better get going if you want to leave with me." I nodded okay.

That was enough to rouse Jack. "Hey! What's happening?" Jack said, sitting up. "Is it time to go? Am I late? It's not even light out yet."

"It's time to get up, dim-wit," I said, after Dad walked out the door. "Hurry up, it's six-thirty. Do you want to shower first?'

"Shower," Jack exclaimed, "Who said anything about taking a shower. I'm not that dirty. Why would I want to clean up now?"

"Gosh, Jack, we're going to meet a whole bunch of people today. Do you want them to think we're a couple of dirty slobs?" He reached in the closet for his pants. "That too, Jack. Are those the only pants you have? They really look dumb. I don't know how you can stand them with the crotch hanging down around your knees. How do you walk without falling down?"

He grumbled, yawning and stretching at the same time. "Man, you sound like my mother. Are you sure you're not related to her?" Then he added in his stupid voice. "Do you want me to wear a suit, Mom? Would that make you happy, Mom?"

I slugged him and headed for the bathroom. "I'll be through in five minutes. Hurry up, you're worse than Andy."

Recognizing his name, Andy opened his eyes a little bit and looked around. Slowly, he stretched and hopped off the bed. Hearing Mom, he headed toward the kitchen, hoping to get a bite of banana or something.

Jack was still on the bed complaining as I went to take a shower. Pretty soon he came in the bathroom. "Don't use all the hot water," he said, before he brushed his teeth.

"Don't worry your head off; Dad fixed the hot water heater yesterday. What's the matter, sissy, you afraid of a little cold water?" He threw a glass of cold water over the shower curtain. "Yow! Brrr! You just wait, Jack. I'm really going to get you for that."

"Oh yeah," Jack said, "What are you going to do?"

"I'm not going to tell you. You just have to know I'm going to get you, and it's going to be bad."

"I'll tell your dad if you do. He wouldn't like you doing something bad to a guest," Jack chided.

"Never mind," I said, "Hand me my towel, will you?"

"What's it worth to you, tough guy?"

I reached out and got my towel. Jack backed up when he saw my arm. "Ha. I saw you flinch. You were afraid I was going to get you—weren't you?"

"No. I was just going to get the towel for you. I was just startled for a second—not afraid."

"Sure you weren't," I laughed, heading for the bedroom. "Hurry up if you want anything to eat." Jack jumped in the shower and was finished in five minutes—he liked to eat.

We got dressed in a hurry. I noticed that Jack had changed into some regular jeans like mine. We just had on tee-shirts, knowing it was going to be hot.

"Morning, Mrs. Matthews, Jack said, as we walked into the kitchen—still sucking up to Mom.

Mom looked around from the stove. "Why good-morning to you, Jack. Did you sleep well?"

"Not bad. That bed's pretty nice."

Dad walked in. "Hi, honey. What's for breakfast?"

"Soft-boiled eggs. I found my egg-cups yesterday. I haven't seen them for years. I didn't know where I had put them; they just came out of one of the boxes. Anyway, I decided to make soft-boiled eggs."

Dad spoke up. "I don't think I've had a genuine soft-boiled egg since you came to visit me in Germany that time. You remember that, don't you?"

Mom gave him a big smile. "Oh, yes. I <u>do</u> remember—everything that happened," she grinned again. "Wasn't that little Gast Haus wonderful?" She had a kind of dreamy look in her eyes.

"I liked those big feather beds," Dad said.

Come on you guys, I thought. Get with it, Mom. We're hungry. "Uh, can I help get anything Mom?" That broke the spell.

"No, Eddie. I've got everything ready to go." She took a plate of toast out of the oven, spooned an egg into each egg-cup, and then served us. "There's more if you're hungry," she said, passing the butter and jam to Dad. "Oh, I almost forgot. Here is our egg-topper, to cut the top off. I got it in Germany, remember?"

She handed it to Dad. It was kind of like a little pair of scissors, except it had a circle instead of blades with a bunch of little cutters that poked out of the inside. He used it and handed it to me. I slid it over the top part of the egg and squeezed. The cutters cracked the shell all the way around, nice and neat. Smiling, I handed it to Jack. "You want to try it."

Jack took them, looking kind of silly. Mom picked up on his problem right away. "Oh, I don't think that Jack has had a soft-boiled egg before. Is that right, Jack?" He nodded and turned a little red. "Help him, Eddie. Show him how to eat it."

"Okay, Mom. It's easy Jack. Once the top is off, you just put your spoon inside the egg and pull out some. I like to mix it up a little and then dip my bread crust in it. Like this, see?"

Jack tried the bread crust method, sticking it in the gooey yoke. He was about to taste it when Dad spoke up. "Those are Humpty Dumpty's brains," he said, grinning. "Good, huh? They'll make you extra smart."

"Ha. That was a good one, Dad." I gave him a thumb up.

Jack dropped the crust. Mom glared at Dad. "Really, Jim. That was awful. Sorry, Jack. Don't pay attention to them. Just take a small bite and then eat some toast. I think you'll like it."

Jack complied. His eyes lit up. "They're pretty good." Mom nodded at him and then gave another glare at Dad and me.

Jack and I both ate two eggs and two pieces of toast. We wanted to be all fueled up for our adventure. Dad was attacking his third egg when we finished—still remembering Germany, I guess. When we were getting up from the table Eddie turned to Dad and said, "Its okay, Mr. Matthews, I knew you were just kidding me about those eggs being brains and all—really. But I won't hold it against you." Mom about choked. With that we ran to our room to get ready.

I said good-bye to Andy, who was getting ready for his morning nap, and we went outside to wait for Dad. It was pretty cool, and I wondered about taking a sweater or a jacket or something. When Dad came out I asked him. "No," he said emphatically, "If anything, you might need to take another tee-shirt, in case that one gets sweaty."

I thought it over, and decided not to take an extra. That would help Mom too, not having to do extra wash. Dad roared off, and we were soon in front of the Lone Star Flying Service. Dad got out. "Come on, you guys, I want you to meet Cody."

We piled out of the car and followed Dad. We walked right into a big hanger that had two airplanes inside. It was kind of dark, since there weren't any flood-lights on. Dad headed for the front left corner where there was a small office built into the end of the hanger. When I walked around a trash can next to the door, I spooked a cat sitting there. Jack almost jumped out of his skin. Just then a kind of a skinny gray-haired guy poked his head out of the door. "What's the ruckus out here? Oh. Hi, Jim. Is this your boy?"

"This is my son, Eddie, and this is his best friend, Jack. Boys, meet the best pilot in Texas, Cody Corbett."

"Howdy, Boys. He stood back and looked at us. "Yessir, Jim," he nodded his head, "Eddie is sure enough your son, you can bet your boots on that—looks just like you—ugly as sin. Ha. Ha." He took off his cowboy hat and whacked his knee. "That's a joke son," he winked at me as he turned to Jack, "An this big feller here seems pretty fine too. Looks like a ball player. I'll bet you're a pitcher, ain't you?" he gave Jack a wink and kind of curled up his lip—at the same time making kind of a double clicking sound. "I want you boys to call me Cody, ya here?" He kind of ran words together—like yessir, instead of yes sir and he made a kind of a whistle when he talked. I think he wore false teeth. "I'll try to keep em out of trouble, Jim. Don't you worry none about them. I'll cuff em if they cause me any grief."

"Thanks Cody, give me a call if you need some relief," Dad said, as he left.

"Not to worry," he yelled after Dad. "Well, boys, let's go find Luis. He can help you get the hang of this place." He popped on his hat and started walking down the hanger door. "Come on if you're comin."

We followed Mr. Corbett—Cody, over to the next hanger. I could see him better now. He wore ironed jeans, cowboy boots, and a light blue shirt. He also wore a big silver belt-buckle with a blue star in the middle, made out of some kind of rock. His hat was kind of silver or tan, or a mixture of each. Anyhow, he looked like a cowboy. The giant doors were open and we walked in. There were three airplanes inside. "That silver one over there is a Cessna 150," Cody said, "this one in the middle is a Cessna 172—see it's got four seats instead of two. Luis should be over there working on that yellow J-3 Super-Cub. Hey, Luis, you here?"

A boy about our size walked out of the rest room. He had on jeans, tennis shoes, and a yellow tee-shirt with a big blue star embroidered on the pocket. "I'm here, Cody. I just finished cleaning up the Cub. I think it's got an oil leak, the cowl was covered—a real mess." Then he spotted us. A big smile came over his face. "One of you must be Eddie. You're dad said you were going to be here soon."

"I'm Eddie," I said, sticking out my hand. This is Jack, my best friend."

He shook hands with me first, and then Jack. "I'm Luis Rodriguez, the only one who works around here," he smiled, took off his baseball cap, and wiped his forehead with his arm.

"That'll be the day," Cody said, grinning, "I pay you way too much for what you do—which ain't much."

Luis stood his ground. "What? You think the starvation wages you pay me is too much? You know I could make a lot more at McDonalds. Heck, I practically run this place."

"Learning how to run the place is part of your pay," Cody answered, giving us a wink. "McDonalds ain't going to teach you nothing about flying, or running things, neither."

"Flying? When's the last time you took me up—I mean for real flying, not just running me over to Tarantula field so I can sit there and sweat all day?"

"Well, maybe I been too busy. I'll get around to giving you some more lessons one of these days."

Luis was getting the upper hand now. "Promise?"

"Well, okay, I promise. You're getting to be a mighty tough arguer, Luis. See, you're learning to be a boss already." He gave Luis a big hug around the shoulder. "Luis is thirteen. He's been working for me since he was a little shaver—about nine, weren't you?"

"Eight," Luis answered, "Seems like longer," he kind of leaned on Cody—just like he was his dad.

"Well compadres, I've got to make a couple of phone calls before the bank tries to close me down. Take good care of these two, Luis. Eddie's dad will kill me if you get them in trouble." Cody turned to leave. "Oh, by the way, Luis, We're going to be busy out at Tarantula next week, maybe the boys would want to go with you." He waved and ambled off toward the office.

"Bye, Cody," we all said in unison.

"Wow, he's something else, I said to Luis. "You like him though, don't you?"

Luis nodded, "He kids around a lot, but he has a heart of pure gold. He's really been good to me and my Mom. He saved us from being deported back to Mexico," he said almost indifferently. "I guess he's been kind of like my second Dad."

"What's deported?" Jack asked.

I jumped in. "It's what they call it when you aren't a citizen, and they send you back to your own country. Right, Luis?"

"Yeah, kind of. It's a long story, but I'll tell it to you while we walk over to Cody's office. I cleaned up that J-3 this morning. All I have to do is fill out the paper work and leave a message for our mechanic to look over the engine for an oil leak. Let's go do that first, and then I'll show you Cody's Lair."

Jack and I walked one on each side of him as we headed off down the ramp. "Thirteen years ago, my real Dad brought my Mom up here just before I was born, from a little town in Durango, Mexico, called Ceballos. She came across the border and had me in a hospital here. That made me an American citizen, but not her. My folks lived here illegally for seven years. Dad was good at building things from stone and brick, so he got plenty of work and was doing real good. Anyway, Cody hired my Dad to build a wall for him, and just before he finished, he got killed in a car accident. That's when the Immigration people tried to send Mom and me back to Mexico. Cody stood up for us and gave Mom a job cleaning up around here, then helped her get the papers to become a citizen. She was sworn in three years ago," he smiled real proud. "Now she's an American, too. Then Cody gave me a job because Mom wasn't able to support us, since she couldn't do much else except be a cleaning woman—which doesn't pay much. And it took her a long time to learn English, so she was limited there too. Anyway, she has a good job now, working for a company that teaches Spanish to Border Patrol Agents. It's right here on the base. That's the story on how I got to know what a good man he is. You can see why I like Cody so much."

"Yeah, he seems like a neat guy," I said. Jack nodded. "Does he have a family or any kids? How old is he?"

"His wife died a long, long, time ago. I think she was killed or something—whatever it was it was bad. He doesn't like to talk about her, so I don't ask. I do know he misses her, though, cause I've caught him looking at her picture sometimes when he sits at his desk. His eyes get all teary when he does. Then he blows his nose and gets back to work. Mom said she thinks his wife was pregnant at the time that he was going to have a son. Maybe that's why he likes kids so much—at least Mom thinks so. I just know he has deep feelings about some things." We arrived at Cody's office and waited while Luis filled out some forms.

Five minutes later, we were back on the ramp. Luis continued his story, "I'm not sure how old Cody is either. I think he must be around seventy. He talks about things he did when he was a kid during World War II. That would make about that old, I think. Anyway, he's in pretty good shape. He can work hard all day, and never seem to get tired. And everybody says he's still the best pilot in Texas. I can't speak to that, cause I haven't flown with anyone else." He kind of let out a deep breath and had a funny look in his eyes.

Then Jack spoke up. "Eddie's dad said he was the best pilot in Texas, too, didn't he Eddie? I nodded. Then Jack looked around. "Well, Luis, what are we going to do next? Are you supposed to be working or something?"

Luis shrugged, "Not really. We're going down there," he pointed to the last hanger in the row. "I want to show you my baby Javelina, and a couple of Cody's toys."

"Keen. That sounds neat," Jack said. "What's a Javelina?"

I cuffed him one on the shoulder "It's a pig," stupid. "You have a real Javelina, Luis? Wow. I heard that they're really mean. Are they?"

Luis nodded his agreement. "I found this little guy out at Tarantula Field. I guess his Mama got killed or something. Anyway, he was pretty weak and hungry, so I brought him back here. I've been feeding him with a bottle. He's doing good, for now, but I'll have to let him go pretty soon. Just because he thinks I'm his mama doesn't mean he's turned nice or something, he's already bit me a couple of times. "Come on, this way."

"You keep mentioning Tarantula Field," I said, as we started walking. "What is it? Another air field?"

"Yeah. This base was originally used to train Air Force jet pilots. They closed it in the sixties—don't know why. Anyway, they had a lot of airplanes when they were open, more than one hundred. Because there was so much congestion here, they needed to use an old World War II Army Air Corps field to practice landings, so they wouldn't overload the local traffic. Tarantula is about thirty miles from here. There's nothing there anymore but an old mobile radio tower, a couple of privies, and three broken down buildings—but it has a seven thousand foot cement runway in perfect shape. Cody bought it when he came to Laredo, and charges private pilots for using it to shoot landings. Actually, he charges two Flying Schools for using it, mainly, one in Hebbronville, and a big school out of San Antonio, Alamo Air. They train pilots to fly corporate jets, Lear Jets mainly. That's how Lone Star got started. Cody bought these first three hangers here, and started a flying school. Then he started taking care of other planes for the local pilots. He has a good operation, and it pays for his toys," he laughed.

"What do you mean, toys? That's the second time you mentioned it."

Luis laughed. "I'll show you after we take care of Porky. He's in here, in Cody's Lair."

There was a big sign painted in yellow and blue on the side of the hanger door: **CODY'S LAIR...enter at your own risk**. Porky must have heard us coming, because there was all kinds of squealing coming from in there.

Luis led us in. It was pretty dark and cool. Heck, it was only about ten in the morning and it must have been eighty-five degrees outside. I guess Dad knew what he was talking about when he said bring an extra tee-shirt. Luis followed the giant sliding door down to the end where the squealing was coming from He had a small wire pen fixed up near the corner. Boy, the noise was getting intense. "Hi, Porky," Luis said, crouching down at the front. A little black pig about the size of a football ran to him, squealing his head off. "Better not touch him," Luis warned us as he went over to a little refrigerator in the corner, retrieving a baby bottle full of milk, "He'll start chewing on your finger if you reach for him." Luis stepped over the side of the pen and sat down in one corner. Porky tried to climb on his lap. After a minute, Luis had the nipple in Porky's mouth and he was slurping away. Heck, he sounded like a giant pig—slurp, slurp, slurp. He was a fast eater, too. When the milk was gone, Porky got mad and tried to bite Luis. Finally, Luis got a hold of him and picked him up. After the screeching died down, he showed Porky to us up close.

"Wow, he already has tusks," Jack said, as Porky made a pass at him.

"And his teeth are like razors," Luis said. "Cody said I should take him back the next time I go to Tarantula. He said the longer I keep him the worse off he'll be, that he would forget what nature planted in him. I guess he already knows how to fend for himself out there. I kind of hate to let him go, but I have to do what's best."

I took a closer look and got snapped at. "Boy, I think Cody's right. He is tough enough to make it out there." Luis stuck him back in the pen.

When the squealing died down he turned to us. "Want to see Cody's toys?"

Luis led us back toward the other end of the Hanger. He stopped by the door and pulled a big old switch. Suddenly, the whole end of the hanger was flooded with light. There in front of me were three of the prettiest airplanes I have ever seen.

WOW! In front was a small low-wing plane with conventional gear—a tail dragger. It wasn't painted, it was just highly polished silver metal. There was a small cockpit with places for two people, side by side. It just looked fast sitting there.

Behind it, in the very back, was another small airplane. It had a two open cockpit configuration with a low wing and conventional gear. The nose was kind of pointed and the engine cylinder-heads, five of them, stuck out of the cowling. The wings and tail were painted yellow, the nose around the engine, blue, and the rest was polished silver metal. It also had military stars on the wings and the tail had red stripes, just like it was painted for the Air Corps in World War II. Golly it was beautiful, and just took my breath away.

Then I spotted a single engine biplane over on the side. It was the neatest one of all, the best looking airplane I have ever seen—it seemed to be flying just sitting there. The lower wings stuck out in front of the top wings, and the plane was really slick looking. It was solid yellow with blue trim.

All of the airplanes looked like they were wet they glistened so much, like they had just been waxed or something. Jack and I just stood there, unable to speak.

"Pretty neat, huh?" Luis said. "This is what Cody lives for. He treats those planes like they were his kids or something. I won't tell you about them, I'll leave that for Cody. He has a story about each one of them, and he's the only one who can tell it right."

"I can hardly wait. Man, these planes are great. I haven't seen anything this exciting since I saw the planets through my neighbor's telescope. What do you think, Jack, aren't they neat?" He didn't answer, he just stood there with his mouth open.

"Hey, it's almost noon," Luis said, checking his watch. Want to go get something to eat at the cafeteria?"

Both of us nodded. I guess we completely forgot about eating with all of the excitement. Jack spoke up, "Is it far? I'm really hungry."

"It's only a couple of blocks." We headed out, and Luis gave us a tour along the way. "These are all of the old buildings that were here when the Air Forced owned the base." He pointed to four or five two story buildings. "Those were called BOQs, (Bachelor Officers Quarters), where the student pilots lived. Those low buildings were for administration. See, there is the old movie theater. The cafeteria is next to it, they just called it a Mess Hall then. The language school where my Mom works is located in that building there," he pointed to the left, "the one with the greenish paint. I think the students live upstairs."

That reminded me. That must be the school that Victoria's aunt runs. "A friend of mine from Homestead has an aunt who runs a language school here. That must be the same one. Let's see, I think her name is Porter—or something like that."

"Virginia Porter. She's the one. Nice lady, Mom says. I guess she can speak a bunch of different languages. She comes down here every summer. Is your friend going to come for a visit?"

"Yes, I think so. Her name is Victoria, she's twelve like us." We turned toward the entrance to the cafeteria.

"What's good to eat here?" Jack asked, as we reached the door.

Luis thought a second. "I think the hamburgers are pretty good—nice and juicy. There's a table over there that's loaded with all kinds of stuff: pickles, peppers, lettuce, tomato, onions, cheese, mustard, catsup, and mayonnaise. You just pick up a plain burger and then put anything you want on it.

"That sounds good to me," Jack said, almost salivating.

"Anything sounds good to you, Jack. Are you sure you're not related to Porky?" That one drew a fist to the arm. "Ouch. Take it easy, Jack. I was just kidding."

"No you weren't."

We all walked through the serving line and selected burgers. Luis was right, they were big and juicy, just like I liked them. I almost got two, but decided on fries instead. I was a sucker for French fries—I could eat a ton of them. Jack got some too, but Luis skipped, taking an apple. Boy, Mom would love him, I thought. Hey, that made me think. Maybe we can have him over for dinner. That would be fun. He could tell Mom all about the place. We got a coke, and then stopped by the table and loaded our burgers with extra stuff. Luis chose a table and we sat down and started eating like crazy. I hoped I didn't sound like Porky. Of course Jack did, but he always sounded that way when he ate. I decided not to say anything, though, we were having too much fun—besides my shoulder was still stinging.

After eating, we messed around for a while looking around the base. Luis pointed out a swimming pool that we could use to cool off when it really got hot in the summer. That was a good idea, maybe I could actually teach Jack how to swim this summer. Now that would be an accomplishment.

———————————

After we finished looking around, we stopped by Cody's office to see if Luis had to do anything. He didn't but we did. Cody said that

Dad had called and wanted to go home at two o'clock, for some reason or other. Heck, it was one-thirty then. Oh Well, It had been a pretty busy day.

Then Cody piped up, "By the way, Boys. I've lined up a Cessna and a Bonanza for you to clean tomorrow. Are you ready to go to work? Luis, do you think you can teach them how?"

Luis grinned. "I guess we'll see tomorrow, right guys?" Then he added. "I think they might learn quicker if you promised to give them a ride in one of your toys."

Cody's eyes lit up. "Did you see my airplanes? What do you think? Do you want to take a ride in one of them?"

"Yes. Yes," we screamed in unison.

"I want to hear your stories about them, too" I added. "Luis said you were the only one that could tell us, and we want to hear. Don't we, Jack?" Jack was still in shock after hearing that we would get a flight in one of his birds, but he managed a nod.

Just then Dad stopped by. "Let's go boys. Thanks, Cody. You too, Luis. I hope they weren't too much bother."

"Not at all Mr. Matthews," Luis said. "We had a good time getting to know each other."

"I'm going to make em earn their keep tomorrow," Cody winked. "We'll see if they're pilot material. They got to learn how to care for them before they can fly them."

Dad smiled and ushered us out the door to his car. "Don't forget your seatbelts," he said, acting like a Dad.

"We won't," we both said in unison, giving each other a knowing nod.

———————————

Jack and I talked a mile a minute, telling Dad about everything that happened. I think he tried to ask a couple of questions, but finally gave up—each of were talking so fast. When we got home, it was Mom's turn. We didn't even complain about setting the table or anything she asked us to do—we even took showers and changed clothes. The only one that lost out was Andy. Poor thing, he kept trying to get attention, but we were too busy talking to Mom—or Dad, whichever one was handy.

Finally, Mom took charge. "Eddie, go feed Andy—now! Then take the pooper-scooper and clean the backyard. Jack, I want you to write a letter to your mom. You can tell her all about the neat things you guys did today. Don't forget to ask her how she is doing at school, and tell her you miss her. Understand?" We both screamed, yes, and hurried off to do our jobs. Dad was back in the kitchen by then and grabbed Mom for a hug and a kiss. I swear those two never quit doing that love-stuff.

By the time we'd finished our projects, Mom called us to dinner. Jack didn't screw up Grace this time, and Mom served right after. "Mmmm. Pork chops and cooked apples, plus roasted red potatoes and peas," I exclaimed. Jack was licking his chops, too. We dug in as soon as Mom sat down.

"This is really good, Mrs. Matthews," Jack said, then wiped his face when Mom's smile turned serious and her eyes concentrated on his mouth. We finished everything in sight, even had seconds on peas. We were checking the table for scraps when Mom brought us giant bowls of chocolate-chip ice cream.

"Go ahead, you two. I know you can't wait for dad and me."

The amount of ice cream was just perfect—lots. It didn't take us long to demolish, but it sure filled us up. I guess Mom could tell, because she let us off the hook for drying the dishes. Sometimes, moms understand when kids need to rest.

After dinner, we went into the living room and sat down. I think all of that food had just about reached our stomachs. Boy were we full. What a day. It was too hot in there, so went out in the back yard and sat on the porch, where we kind of went over our day in detail.

Andy joined us after Mom put the food away. He begged a quick tummy rub, and then curled up to take his after dinner nap. Suddenly, he let out a yip, and ran to the Armadillo's hole—razing cane. Jack stood back while I crouched down and looked inside. I saw something move and heard a little scratching sound. "Hey, Mom. Do you have any eggs? I need a couple for our Armadillo, he's moving around again."

Mom came to the door with a couple of eggs. "Don't let Andy get it," she said, retreating back to the kitchen, "He might hurt the poor little thing."

Jack spoke up, "Poor little thing? Doesn't she know it's a wild animal? It might even be bigger than Andy." He stood there looking at the hole from about ten feet away.

I rolled the eggs down the hole. "No. He…it…whatever, is probably pretty small, actually. Heck, they're mostly shell."

"Shell? They have a shell?" Jack just stood there, dumbfounded.

"Sure. Boy, Jack, for a twelve-year-old, you sure don't know much. Come on, I'll show you a picture of one in my nature book. And quit being so nervous, they wouldn't harm a flea."

"But I thought you said they were bug eaters. Fleas are bugs, aren't they?"

That one wasn't even worth an answer. "Come on, dummy."

CHAPTER EIGHT

We were up at six the next morning, and had an uneventful breakfast—Jack was getting used to things, and he didn't even try to put on those stupid pants—guess he learned from yesterday that no one wore them around here. Dad dropped us off at the Lone Star Flying Service about seven fifteen. Luis showed up about ten minutes later.

"Good morning, you guys," he said, yawning, "I just can't seem to get going this morning."

"Me neither," I said, answering his yawn, "I thought I slept good, but maybe I didn't."

Jack looked at both us with astonishment. "I'm ready for a little adventure. What's wrong with you? You guys act like old people."

Luis answered. "Well, I don't think that cleaning up two dirty airplanes is exactly an adventure. I call that work."

I guess he knew what he was talking about. "Is it that much work?" I asked. "I thought it might be kind of fun, for us anyway."

Luis thought a minute. "Yeah, I guess it could be fun. At least I thought it was fun the first few times I did it. But now, it's just plain old work." He yawned again. "Well, let's get going, the sooner we start, the sooner we'll finish. At least that what Cody says. Uh, maybe you guys want to take off your shirts. You are probably going to get a little wet from the sprayer."

After stripping off our shirts, we headed off for the middle hanger where the Bonanza and the Cessna were parked. Jack and I were kind of excited about working on real airplanes. Luis wasn't, it was like mowing the grass to him.

I knew what a Cessna looked like, a high wing all metal airplane. This one was a 150, a two seat model. The other one, the Bonanza, was really different. It had a low wing and a really funny tail—just a V, not the usual rudder and elevator configuration—and it had retractable gear. It was also all metal, seated four, and had a lot of extra instruments. Luis said it was an all weather airplane—that it could fly in almost any weather conditions. The Cessna was strictly for visual flight. I was starting to get the hang of the airplane lingo, at least I understood VFR (visual flight rules), and IFR (instrument flight rules). It made sense that you didn't go flying around in clouds or at night without having the proper instruments—like the artificial horizon that Dad showed Jack and me.

Luis took charge. "First we vacuum out the cockpits, then dust them with this spray stuff. Then you clean the inside of the windows. This stuff, here, is special for Plexiglas. Make sure you really polish the windshield good with this soft cotton cloth. Then, I'll get the power sprayer and wash down the outsides. We just dry them a little with these old towels, and let the air do the rest. When they're dry, we polish the outside of the Plexiglas and put armor-all on the tires. I'll clean the propellers with this spray wax. That's it."

"That's a lot," Jack said, wiping his forehead. "Whew, I got tired just listening to you."

"Hold it, Jack," I responded, "Just think, Luis normally does this all by himself. Heck, we'll be done before you know it."

Jack shrugged. "I guess it's not so bad."

Luis gave us a pep talk. "Let's get going, guys. The sooner we're finished, the sooner we can mess around."

I grabbed one of the vacuums. "I'll do the Bonanza. Jack, you get the Cessna. Let's get this over with." We went right to work and the job went pretty fast, in spite of the fact that this was the first time Jack and I had cleaned an airplane. Before we knew it, we were wiping down the wet aircraft. Jack polished the Cessna windows and I took the Bonanza again. Luis finished the wheels and was polishing the propellers by the time we finished.

Luis looked at his watch. "Hey, two hours and forty minutes for two planes, that's a new record. Boy, we make a good team. By the way, did Cody tell you how much we get for this?"

"No," Jack and I said in unison, perking up at the sound of money.

"Well, Cody normally charges $100.00 per airplane, and only keeps what it costs for the supplies and towels. I think we should get at least $50.00 apiece."

"Fifty bucks apiece," Jack and I exclaimed. "Yeah." We all danced around, celebrating our good luck by acting like nuts.

Then I got to thinking about all of that stuff on the instrument panel in the Bonanza. "Luis, do you know much about the instruments? I thought maybe you could explain them to us, so we know what Cody is saying when he takes us up."

Then I got to thinking about all of that stuff on the instrument panel in the Bonanza. "Luis, do you know much about the instruments? I thought maybe you could explain them to us, so we will understand what Cody is saying when he takes us up."

"Okay, but first I need to give you a lesson about why airplanes fly, and how the controls work, then I'll cover the different instruments—both engine and flight. I'll show you using this model airplane and the chalkboard over there." We walked over and sat down while Luis stood in front of us. "The reason an airplane flies is because of the wing shape, called an airfoil." He held up the model and drew a cross-section of an airfoil on the blackboard. It was what you would see if you cut a slice out of the wing. You notice the bottom of the wing is almost straight from front to back, and the top of the wing curves up near the front and gradually drops down to meet the bottom?" We both nodded. "Well it is that curve that gives the aircraft lift. The relative wind must move faster to follow the curve on the top than it does on the bottom. For example, two air molecules split at the leading edge of the wing. The molecule passing over the curved part on top has to travel a greater distance than the molecule traveling along the bottom, which is straight. Therefore, it has to travel faster to reach the trailing edge of the wing at the same time. There is a Law of Physics, sometimes called Bernoulli's Principle, which says: 'as speed increases, pressure decreases.' This means that the increased velocity of the air across the top causes lower pressure on the top, no matter what speed you fly. The lower pressure on the top of the wing opposes the gravitational pull on the weight of the airplane, and is why we call it lift. The more the upper surface is curved, the more lift is produced at a given speed. That's why airliners extend the flaps on the trailing edge of the wing, to create more curvature in the wing." He showed us how the air moved on the airfoil diagram on the blackboard, and how the distance the air traveled moved when the flaps were lowered. "Another way to create lift is to increase the angle of attack, by tilting the front of the wing upward." He showed us how the air moved on the airfoil diagram he drew on the blackboard. "You have probably noticed that airliners tilt the nose up as they slow down to land. That is important, because the center of gravity (CG) has to be within the limits of the center of lift. In other words, the weight of the heavy engine needs to be closer to the center of lift than the lighter tail in order to keep the CG within the forward and aft limits, or you will run out of elevator control at slower airspeeds. He demonstrated with the model how it would run out lift. "See how this model balances when I hold it by the wing tips?"

Seeing our confusion, he ran through the whole thing again. After the second time we both just sat there for a minute with our mouths open. "Wow." Jack and I both exclaimed, and nodded at the same time when we finally understood the concept.

Luis continued. "Now that you understand the basics of lift, there are four more things that you need to understand: Power, Pitch, Roll, and Yaw. Power is easy. You need something to pull or push the aircraft forward so the wing can produce lift and start flying. On smaller planes, the propeller causes the plane to move, kind of like the gears move the wheels in a car. The throttle controls the speed of the propeller like the gas-peddle in a car. The more throttle you add, the faster the propeller turns. Do you understand?"

We both answered yes simultaneously. "Okay, now I will demonstrate pitch. This horizontal part of the tail is the elevator. It moves the aircraft nose up or down depending on which way you move the controls. I know you have put your hand out of a car window and felt the relative wind push your hand up or down." We both nodded and smiled at each other. Luis continued. "The same thing happens when you move the flight control stick forward or back." He moved close to us and demonstrated how the elevator worked on the model. We both got it at the same time and started nodding like crazy.

Luis smiled, happy that he was getting through to us. "Roll is a little difficult to understand, as it ties in with lift and power. When you want to turn left, you move the stick to the left. That moves the ailerons, the small control surfaces near the end of the wing. In a left turn, the left aileron moves up into the low-pressure area on top of the wing and spoils some of the lift, causing the wing to drop. At the same time, the right aileron moves down into the high-pressure area below the wing. This in effect increases the wing chord, which increases the lift, causing the right wing to rise. However, this action also causes an increase in right wing drag, which we call 'adverse yaw,' and must be countered with left rudder to coordinate the turn. When you reach the number of degrees of bank you want, you center the stick. That is how an airplane turns. To stop the turn you do just the opposite, by pushing the stick to the right until you are wings level. Since the lift vector changes during a turn, you will have to apply a little backpressure and add power to prevent the airplane from losing altitude and airspeed." Again, he had to show us a couple of times before we understood.

Luis noticed when we finally got it and smiled. "The next movement is called yaw. Yaw is when the rudder moves back and forth like this." He demonstrated using the model. "You never want to turn by yawing the aircraft because it increases parasite drag (also known as adverse yaw), which interrupts the center of pressure. Remember when I talked about this kind of yaw?"

"That was when you talked about roll, and why you didn't just point the nose to a heading by using rudder." Jack said.

"You're right, Jack. That is why you roll into a turn, coordinate with the rudder, and by letting the change in lift vector pull you around the turn. A good pilot always wants the aircraft to fly smoothly through the air without drag. You already know that the foot pedals in the cockpit control the rudder, and you can tell if the aircraft is in a yaw by crosschecking an instrument called the turn and slip indicator. To maintain level flight, pitch and yaw the must be checked constantly using the horizon as a gauge. Of course power is important too, because adding power increases the airflow over the wings, and the results are increased lift and drag. You have to push the nose down or change the trim when you add power, because the negative lift on the elevator increases and causes the nose to rise. Keep in mind that as airspeed increases drag increases. You will learn about all of this when you get your first real flight lesson, and learn how to use the rudder differently when landing in a crosswind.

It was a bit confusing but we both pretty much understood. Then Jack blurted out, "Eddie's dad taught us about level flight, only he showed us how to do it on an artificial horizon. Which one is best?"

"Mr. Matthews is right; the artificial horizon instrument is more accurate. That is why it is used when you are flying in weather."

Jack elbowed me, "Remember, your dad told us that too."

I shushed him, and returned my attention to Luis. "If the artificial horizon is more accurate, why don't you use it all of the time?"

"Because when you are flying a small plane close to the ground you need to be alert for radio towers and other aircraft, and keep your eyes peeled for them at all times. You will be surprised how fast you can tell whether or not you are straight and level just by using the horizon; the real one, not the instrument. It takes a while before you learn to spot other planes flying around and you need to learn how as fast as possible. A mid-air collision can ruin your whole day," he joked. "Come on," Luis said, putting down the model. "That is enough about basic flying. After you start flying you will go over these principals a thousand times and understand them just as well as I do—Cody will see to that. Let's go over to the Cessna and I will explain the engine instruments."

We spent the next half hour going over the main engine instruments in the Bonanza and Cessna. "I'll cover the flight instruments the next time. If I went over them now, you would probably forget everything I said. There are just too many instruments to cover in one sitting." Both Jack and I agreed. The session about basic flying that Luis presented had been super, and I was excited about getting my first real flying lesson. Jack felt the same way. I could tell because of the way he walked—confident in the way he swaggered.

I stood up. "Thanks, Luis, I really learned a lot about flying today. Boy, we sure have got a lot to learn. There is more to flying than I thought."

"You are a good teacher," Jack said. I agreed with Jack and thanked Luis again.

Luis agreed, and we spent the next half hour going over the main engine instruments in the Bonanza and Cessna. "I'll cover the flight instruments the next time. If I went over them now, you would probably forget everything I said. There's too many instruments to cover in one sitting." Both Jack and I agreed.

"Well, what do you want to do for the rest of the day?" Luis asked. We both just stood there and looked at each other, but didn't know what to suggest. Seeing our predicament, Luis made a proposal. "Would you like to go over to Lake Casa Blanca. It's only a mile or so on the other side of the runways, and we can probably hitch a ride. There's a neat little park and a lot of big old rocks to climb around on. Then we also watch the water skiers and look at their boats,

"Keen," Jack said, then checked his watch. "Can you get anything to eat over there. It's almost eleven."

"Sure. There's a couple of hot dog stands, but they sell other snacks too. They aren't great, but, they're not bad."

"Let's go Amigos," Jack hollered.

Luis looked at him kind of funny, then smiled. "I guess I could teach you guys a little Spanish. I'll just point out different things and tell you what they're called in Spanish. It's better to learn the names of things first, then you can start studying the grammar part."

"*Gracias, Senior,*" Jack said, real proud of himself.

Luis chuckled. "*Vamos, amigos. El Lago esta ahi,*" He pointed the way. "*Vamos* means, let's go. *Lago* means, lake. *Esta ahi*, means, it is over there." We must have looked kind of dumb because he added, "Don't try and remember specific words, just repeat them and eventually the meanings will sink in."

Off we went on another adventure. We were finding out that there was more stuff to do here than we'd imagined.

We hooked a ride with the local Texas Park Ranger. His name was Jimmy Thornton. He didn't work just here, he was responsible for a bunch more public parks along the Rio Grande, River. Anyway, I'm glad we caught a ride, it was further than I thought.

The first thing we did after we arrived was get a hot dog. Jack was about to keel over from the lack of food. The hot dogs weren't great, just like Luis said, but they took away the hunger pangs. Afterwards, we wandered down around the docks to look at the boats. They were mostly speed boats used for water skiing—slick looking, noisy, and fast. Then, we fooled around the gigantic rocks that lined the lake on the northwest end. "Careful," Luis said, as we wandered between the boulders. "There are quite a few rattlesnakes around here. Look where you step." Jack instantly came to attention—me too. "They won't strike unless you step on them, or kick at them," he added, seeing our concern. "I guess you aren't used to having snakes around." He paused a minute, "You should though. Didn't you know that there are more rattlesnakes in Florida than in Texas? And that there a zillion other kinds there that are poisonous?"

I was shocked. "What! You're kidding, right?"

"No, my science teacher told me. There are tons of water moccasins in Florida, and lots of copper-heads, too. They also have the two most poisonous snakes in America, the coral snake and the eastern rattler."

"Wow," Jack said. "I didn't know that. Did you know that, Eddie?"

"No. I knew we had a lot of snakes down there, but I didn't imagine there were more than in Texas. Texas is so big."

"There's also a lot more water in Florida, which snakes like." Luis, offered, that's why the rattlesnakes hang around the lake.

"Stop! Luis! What's that?" Jack pointed at something on the corner of a good sized rock.

Luis took a cautious look, then smiled. "That's a tarantula. There are a million of them around here. That's why they call our auxiliary runway, Tarantula Field. When I take you out there we can watch them—they're kind of interesting. You won't believe what happens after they mate."

"Spiders mate?" Jack asked.

"Sure, dummy. All things mate. How do you think they have babies?" I shook my head. "Some times I wonder about you, Jack. What happens, Luis?"

"You'll have to wait," he laughed, "I'll let you see for yourself."

By this time Jimmy had made his rounds and was headed for the other side. He spotted us sitting on a huge rock, resting. "You guys want a lift back?" he hollered.

"You're a lifesaver, Mr. Thornton," Jack said, getting up, thinking about that mile and a half walk to the base.

"Everything okay, Jimmy?" Luis asked, as we climbed in his van.

"Just fine. The rest rooms are all working—that's the main thing. You can't believe how much criticism we get when a bathroom is out of order. That's the biggest complaint we have. Seems like I've got a plumber out here once a week. My biggest concern is the water level, it's about eighteen inches low. But no one else seems to notice that. Of course I couldn't do anything about the rain if I wanted to." He chuckled to himself. It must have been kind of a private joke, I figured, since it wasn't very funny.

———————————

Cody met us when we got back to the office. "Good job on those planes, boys. The owners seemed happy enough, leastwise. They left you a little tip—$10.00 each. Here's your pay, $65.00 apiece. Now don't run out and spend it on something dumb, y'all should put a little of it away—save it for a rainy day."

We all thanked him in unison. I can't remember when I held that much money in my hand.

I think we were wearing the biggest smiles that ever crossed our face when Cody spoke up again. "Eddie, Jack. Would you be up to taking a little spin in the PT-22 tomorrow morning?"

I couldn't believe what he said. Jack looked at me with the same surprised expression that I must have been showing. Then we started nodding, and were finally able to speak. "You bet, Cody," we screamed, jumping up and down, slugging each other. Luis told us that he'd see us in the morning and left for home. We just stood there, grinning like crazy, wondering what we were in for.

Finally, Cody interrupted our glee. "Hold it, boys, settle down for a minute. Since Mr. Matthews isn't going to pick you up for a couple of hours, I thought we might amble down to the Lair and I'll get you ready for your flight tomorrow. Is that all-right with you?"

We quieted down real quick. "Yes, Sir, Cody," we said together.

"Then, let's go." He took off for the hanger, really moving out, not ambling like he said.

We took off after him, and ended up walking with him stride for stride, one on each side. He walked pretty fast for an old guy, and we actually had to hurry to keep up. When we arrived at the Lair, he flipped on the light switch and led us to the Ryan trainer in the back of the hanger.

Boy, the airplane was really neat. "Okay, listen up," Cody said. "This little bird was built in late 1941. They had always used biplanes as primary trainers before 1940, the PT-17, but they didn't fly the same as the newest fighters, so they came up with the PT-22. It was really a pretty hot airplane for it's day. This little baby will do 125 miles per hour, and will perform every acrobatic maneuver in the book. It's a little tricky at times, especially on the ground, it being a tail dragger, but it taught our boys what to expect when they went into fighters. This bird is powered by a 160 horse power Kinner engine, it has a wing span of thirty feet, and is almost twenty-one feet long. It only weighs a little over eighteen hundred pounds. I think it is one of the best airplanes ever built." He smiled, and kind of patted the aircraft near the engine. "You guys will have to wear parachutes, of course, because we are going to do some aerobatics."

We must have looked scared, because he tried to settle us down. "I don't want you to worrying about it being dangerous, it ain't, and it's just that the FAA requires us to wear chutes. Heck, you only use one in case of a real emergency, and I never had one of those I couldn't get out of." Both Jack and I looked suspiciously at each other with that remark, still a little unsure. Cody acted real calm, though, and said we wouldn't have a problem, because this was the best PT-22 in the world, and it was in the best condition a mechanic could make it. "I want to take you through some acrobatics: rolls, loops, and that kind of stuff. You won't have any problems after you experience a couple—it's really fun. I have headsets in this bird, they used to have only a voice tube. I'll show you what that is—it's still in the airplane. Anyway, I'll tell you everything I'm going to do before hand, so you don't have to worry that I am going to surprise you."

He looked at us, smiling. " Okay, come on over to this chair, and I'll fit you with chutes. He took a parachute out of a locker and placed it on the seat of the chair. This is a butt-pack, you sit on it." Jack went first. "Okay, put your arms through here. Fine, that's about right," he said as he hooked the chest clamp and pulled on some adjustment straps. He grabbed two leg straps, and did some adjusting first, then hooked it up to some side clamps and pulled on one of the straps. The chute tightened right up around Jack's legs and waist. "Now these straps are important, you want them real tight. So after you sit down in the cockpit, you will need to pull down on these straps and cinch them up tight. Got it?" Jack nodded. He helped Jack out of the chute and I took my turn. "Good, you guys are about the same size in the torso. There's hardly any adjusting to do." He unbuckled the chute. "Okay, up you go. I'm going to stick this chute in the front cockpit where you guys will be. Come on, Eddie, hop in and I'll point out a few things." He showed me how to adjust the seat height and where the headset and voice tube were located. He showed me how to adjust the rudder pedals and pointed out the airspeed, altimeter, and artificial horizon. Jack came next, and Cody repeated the lesson. "Well, if you understand, let's head back to the office." We both nodded. We asked him a couple of things during the walk over to the office, but mainly, we were too excited to think of any good questions. We just followed him in awe.

Just then Dad drove up. Cody gave a wave and opened his office door. "I'll see you in the morning, guys. We'll probably takeoff around eight-thirty. You can flip for who goes first. I'll brief you on how to use the chutes just before you fly, then you won't forget."

We waved goodbye to Cody and jumped in the car. Both of us were too excited to speak.

Then Dad broke the silence. "What's going on, you two, don't I even get a hello?"

"Hello, Dad."

"Hello, Mr. Matthews."

Dad pulled over. "Okay, what is it? I'm not moving until you tell me." We both started at once, then Dad waved for us to quiet down. "Wait. Wait. Eddie, you first."

"Cody is going to take us up in the PT-22 tomorrow morning."

Dad's eyes lit up. "No kidding," he broke out in a big smile. "No wonder you two are totally out of it." Then he leaned back, kind of like he was in a trance. "Boy, it's been a long time since I did any real acrobatics. Wow! What a way for you to get your first real taste of the skies, in a famous open cockpit World War II primary trainer with the best pilot in Texas. Man, I envy you guys."

We both started to talk at the same time again, but I let Jack go first. "We got fitted out for parachutes and everything." Then he thought for a second. "But that doesn't mean we are going to need them or anything. Cody said we wouldn't. Right, Eddie?"

"Right. And we are going to fly in the front cockpit, isn't that neat?" I added.

Dad thought about what we had just said. "Uh, maybe you shouldn't mention the parachutes to your Mother. You know how moms are sometimes, about things like that." We both nodded. "And I think we need to call your mom, Jack, to let her know you're going to fly. To kind of get her consent—just in case...."

"In case of what?" I asked. Jack looked worried. Then it sunk in. "What if Mom won't let me fly because she thinks it is too dangerous?" I said.

Now Jack really looked worried. "If you're mom's scared, then my mom will go nuts." He hunkered down in the seat, really dejected.

Dad kind of chose his words carefully. "Well, boys, it's always a good idea to let moms in on these kinds of decisions. Trust me. It's when you don't tell them that things get screwed up. Why, I'm sure that they will be really excited for you, and have no problems with you flying at all."

"But what if they do have a problem? Jack said, now looking worse.

Dad looked determined. "Don't worry. Let me talk to Janet about it after we get home. You two can go to your bedroom to clean up while I talk with her—kind of grease the skids, so to speak." He was nodding to himself, as he said it, full of confidence. "Everything will work out fine." That comment made Jack look more worried. Me too, I always had my doubts when Dad got involved in something important about me with Mom.

Just like Dad suggested, we went straight to the bedroom when we got home. Jack insisted we had to flip for who was first in the shower. I told Jack he could have his choice, but he said we had to flip. Guess who won, again? Then he couldn't make up his mind whether or not to go first or second. I told him I was getting a little tired of flipping all the time. "Why don't we just take turns?"

"Because we agreed to do it the first day I got here, that's why. Besides, I kind of like flipping. I'll go first," he decided at last. He ripped off his clothes, dumped them in a pile on the floor, and headed for the shower.

As he was walking out the door I yelled. "Hey, Jack, what year was it when you were born?" I was hoping to catch him saying 1991, which would make him eleven.

"Same as you, dummy, 1990. We're only one month a part, remember?"

Well, I thought, either he's exceptionally quick in math—which he isn't—or he really is twelve. Who knows, maybe he's just a young twelve.

Our showers went okay, and we put on our best everyday clean clothes. I picked out a shirt that Mom liked—couldn't hurt. "Make sure you comb your hair, Jack," I reminded him. "We don't need Mom to make her think we aren't responsible."

"Good idea," Jack said, going back for a little touch up.

I checked my watch. We'd been home for almost thirty minutes. That should be enough time for Dad to work on Mom, I figured. We walked into the kitchen. "Hi, Mom," I said, giving her a little hug—boy you smell good.

"Hi, Mrs. Matthews," Jack mimicked my compliment, "Boy, you sure look nice tonight."

Oh no! Man, he's really sucking up. Now she'll know for sure that we want something.

Dad chimed in. "Boys, I told Janet that Cody wants to take you for a flight tomorrow. I told her that Cody briefed you for over an hour on all of the safety procedures, and thinks you're ready for your first flight. I think she's about as excited about it as you are."

Mom rolled her eyes. "Are you guys working on me or something? Look at you boys, dressed in your best clean clothes, hair combed. I'll bet you even brushed your teeth. Even Jim is giving me the hard sell. What is it that you don't want me to know?"

"Parachutes," Jack blurted out. If looks could kill, Jack would have been in a heap on the floor.

Dad and I took a deep breath when Mom turned around. "Parachutes?"

Dad stepped in. "It's just a requirement by the FAA. Cody is going to show them some mild aerobatics and he has to follow the rules. It's really nothing." He glared at Jack.

"If it's nothing, then why didn't you tell me in the first place?" Mom busied herself with dinner, a sure sign of concern for us.

We all just stood there, waiting for her to say something. The silence was awful. Then she turned around. "Look, Boys," she looked right at Dad when she said it, "If Jim tells me Cody is a good pilot and a safe pilot, I trust his judgement. I know how important this is to you. But I have to bring Caroline into the loop, she needs to know—she has to have a say in this. I will call her, and tell her that Jim thinks it is completely safe. Don't worry, Jack, I think she will trust Jim too. Mom's just worry about their children, in spite of the fact that you think you've already grown up. Mom's think their children always need their help, no matter how big you are. So give us a break, here." Dad grabbed her and they hugged. There they go again, I thought, wondering how long it would take before she called Jack's mom.

We ate dinner right away. I can't even remember what we had, or whether it was good. We even volunteered to dry the dishes, to help hurry up Mom's call to Florida. Finally, she was done in the kitchen and went into her bedroom. I guess she was going to call from in there. Jack and I were chewing our fingernails off by the time she stuck her head out the door. "Jack, you're mom wants to talk to you for a minute."

Jack just sat there frozen for a minute, then slowly got up and went into Mom's bedroom. Now, it was time for Dad and I to chew on our nails. A couple of minutes later, Jack came running out, acting like a crazy man. "She said it was okay," he exclaimed. We hugged each other and danced around.

Mom came out. "Boys, it think you ought to get a good nights sleep if you are going to do all of those acrobatics tomorrow."

We ran for our bedroom and jumped onto our beds. "Tomorrow is going to be the neatest day in my life," Jack said from the top bunk.

"Mine too," I said. Andy joined us and curled up on his pillow at the foot of the bed. I think he knew that everything was all-right. Somehow, he always knew.

CHAPTER NINE

———

We slept pretty good until four in the morning. Then Jack and I just laid there and listened to the clock tic for the rest of the night—morning—whatever. Finally, I heard Dad get up. It must be six, I decided. Then I heard Jack, breathing away up there on the top bunk, sounding like a steam engine. "You awake, Jack?"

He bounced around in his bed. "Is it time to get up?" he asked, having a little hopeful sound in his voice.

"Almost," I said, waiting for Dad to walk out of his bedroom to the kitchen." Finally he did, and we piled out of bed. Andy just lay there, wondering what was going on. We showered and dressed in record time, then hurried to the kitchen. Mom had joined Dad by the time we were ready, and was cooking some bacon and making toast.

She grinned at us. "Are you boys excited?"

What kind of question was that, I wondered. We were getting ready for the neatest experience in our lifetimes, and she asks us that. Jack even looked at me in wonderment. I answered thought, just to be polite. "Yes' Mom. We're excited."

"Sit down. I made you bacon and scrambled eggs." We pulled out our chairs. Dad joined us quickly—he liked bacon and eggs too.

She served, and we quickly dug in. None of us said a thing. We just concentrated on eating. Finally Dad broke the silence. "This is a wonderful breakfast, Janet. I hope the boys fly more often." She ignored his remark.

"Me too," Jack said, "I mean about flying. And the breakfast too, Mrs. Matthews—it's great." There he goes, sucking up again. Oh well, Mom seemed to like it. I guess Dad an I didn't compliment her enough, being so used to her and everything.

"Any more toast, Mom?" I asked, then added quickly, "I think it's the best breakfast I ever ate."

Mom smiled and handed me another piece. "Anyone else? How about more jam?"

The others gladly accepted and gobbled down the toast. Then Dad checked his watch. "Ah oh, it's time to go. I hope you guys don't get sick after eating that big breakfast," he said as he got up, "You'd make an awful mess in that plane." He was grinning until he saw Mom.

Did he mean throw-up I wondered? Jack wondered too, I could see him starting to worry. Mom gave Dad a quick glare and shook her head. "Sometimes I wonder about you, Jim."

Dad didn't answer, he just ran for it. "Come on guys. I was just kidding. You won't have any trouble." We didn't look too confident, I guess, so he added, "You didn't get sick on the Gulfstream, did you?" I looked at Jack and could tell Dad's comment helped ease his mind. It didn't help me, however, I knew that riding in the Gulfstream wasn't anything like doing loops and stuff.

Then Dad reminded us, "You'd better run in and get a sweat shirt or heavy sweater. It may be hot on the ground, but it gets much cooler at five thousand feet."

We ran for our bedroom and grabbed two sweatshirts. "Did you hear that? Five thousand feet. Wow! That's way up there," Jack said, starting to pull on his shirt.

"That may be a little early, Jack. We don't even go up for over and hour, and you might not even go first—we still have to flip."

He took off the shirt. "When do you want to flip? How about now?"

"Okay," I said, pulling out my nickel. "You call it."

I flipped the nickel and let it fall on the floor. "Heads," Jack called, holding his fingers crossed." The coin rolled around for a while before it finally fell over. "It's heads! It's heads! I'm first!" Then Jack did his usual thing, jumping up an down like an idiot.

"Let's go, boys," Dad hollered, "Almost time for you to hit the blue."

Mom waylaid us at the door and gave us both a hug. "Be careful you two. And listen to what Cody says. Have fun."

"Thanks," we yelled as we ran for the car and jumped in, making sure that we hooked up our belts—kind of like practicing for when we were in the airplane. Dad hooked his, and we headed out for our best adventure ever.

————————————

When we got to Cody's, the PT-22 was sitting out front of the hanger, shining like crazy in the morning sun. Luis was already there, checking out something by the engine. Dad hopped out of the car and walked over to the plane with us. He stopped at the left wing for a minute and just ran his hands up and down over the skin, and then hopped up and looked into the cockpit. "Hi, Mr. Matthews," Luis said. "You got any time in one of these?"

Dad shook his head. "Nope. Wish I did. The nearest thing I've flown that's close to this baby was a T-34. A friend of mine was running a flying service out of a Meecham Field, in Ft Worth. They took people up and did a little of air-to-air combat—to give them a thrill. It was lots of fun, but I'm sure it was nothing like this." Luis gave him a nod, like he understood.

Just then Cody came out of his office carrying a couple of old leather flying helmets, goggles and all. "Is the bird ready, Luis?" he hollered, getting a thumbs up for an answer. "How about trying these on the boys while I talk with Mr. Matthews." He tossed the helmets to Luis. "Hi, Jim," Cody said, shaking hands. "Think the boys are ready for this? Did they get any sleep last night? They were awful excited when they left yesterday." They looked over at us standing over by the end of the wing.

Dad laughed. "I don't know, Cody, but I know how they feel. I think I'm as excited as they are."

"Guess you ain't got any time in an open two-holer like this one," he said, clapping Dad on the back. He didn't give him a chance to answer before Cody continued. "If you can make it back around ten-thirty, I'll give you a chance to see what it's like—give you a quick spin after I fly Luis. There'll still be enough gas for you to do a few things—how's a snap-roll sound? It's probably been a while."

Dad's eyes lit up. "I'll make time somehow, Cody. Thanks. I think I'll run over to your office and call in. Maybe they can do without me until noon. I want to watch the kid's too, if I can." He hurried off.

Luis had us try on the helmets and adjusted the chin-straps and goggles. Cody reached over and pulled his helmet out of the back cockpit. "Okay, boys. Which one of you is going to be first?"

Jack held up his hand and Cody helped him in the front cockpit. He made sure the parachute straps were tight and then cinched down the seat-belt and shoulder-harness, and pointed out the rip-cord— telling him when to pull it if there was a real emergency. He plugged in the intercom-cord and then jumped in the back cockpit, repeated the procedure on himself.

At that point he gave Luis a spinning signal with his hand.. Luis, who was standing by the engine, turned a small crank a few turns and then gave Cody a thumbs-up signal. "Let her rip," Cody yelled. Luis did something and the prop spun over a few times, then the engine started with a big puff of smoke—brroom. Jack gave us a wave from the front cockpit. In a minute or so, Cody gave a signal for Luis to pull the wheel-chocks. Then Cody revved up the engine and they headed out toward the taxiway.

I went over to Dad. He gave me a squeeze on the shoulder and we watched them as they lined up and took-off. The engine really sounded cool as the little airplane tore into the air. It made a right turn at the end of the runway and climbed toward the east. Darn, I thought, I wish had made the call on that flip. Right then, I wanted to be first.

Dad and I just stood there looking where Cody and Jack had gone, before the plane disappeared into the brightness of the rising sun. We couldn't see the airplane, but we could hear the engine noise, especially when they were in a dive. I started getting nervous about my turn. I tried not to think about getting sick—how embarrassing would that be?

Thirty minutes after they had left, Luis hollered, "Here they come." I guess he knew right where to look. Then I saw the little plane speeding toward the airport.

"I see it. There they are, headed for the runway kind of low," I pointed the plane out to Dad. He gripped my shoulder and nodded. They made a sweeping turn onto final approach and landed. My mouth was feeling kind of dry as I watched them taxi in.

Luis told me Cody was going to leave the engine running, and to put on my helmet and buckle the chin-strap—then he'd help me into the cockpit. "I'll make sure everything is buckled up," he said reassuringly, then briefed me on the rip-cord. All I could do was nod.

Cody made a big swing around, gunning the engine just before coming to a stop. Luis jumped up on the wing and helped Jack get out, then he grabbed my hand and pulled me up. The next thing I remember was being in the cockpit and Luis was giving me a thumbs-up. "Hey, Eddie, it's me, Cody. Can you hear me?"

"I hear you fine, Cody," I said, hearing my voice sounding kind of different.

"Okay, Cowboy, let's go." He gunned the engine and we surged ahead. He made S-turns while he taxied so he could see in front of him. The nose gets in the way when you are in the back seat of a tail-dragger.

All of a sudden we were at the end of the runway and the tower gave us a green light. Then I realized that the airplane didn't have a radio, just an intercom. "Here we go," Cody said. The engine roared. We bounced along for only a couple of seconds, it seemed, and then we were in the air, climbing fast. We turned out over Lake Casa Blanca and headed east. He just kept climbing until we hit six thousand feet. "Okay, Eddie, I am going to do a couple of steep turns to get you used to maneuvering around, then I'll do an aileron roll. After we finish that, we'll do a loop and a couple of other fun maneuvers. How do you feel?"

"I'm fine, Cody," I said, hardly able to speak. He pushed the throttle up and the engine revved up pretty good. Then we suddenly made a really steep left turn.

"How was that?" he asked.

"Great," I said, really meaning it.

"Okay, Cowboy, let's let her rip." He nosed it over a little and the engine roared even louder. Then he pulled the nose up and we made a roll to the left. It was funny, I thought to myself, it's like the whole sky was rolling, not us. Then Cody whipped the plane over and put it into a pretty steep dive. When the engine was really howling, he pulled the nose up. It didn't stop at the horizon, it just kept going right past straight up, then upside down, then to straight down, where Cody started to pull out. I sunk down in the seat and my head felt really heavy. I could hardly move my arms either. "You're feeling gravity forces pulling on you, Eddie. Right now, you weight almost three times your normal weight." I tried to talk but I couldn't. We didn't stop at the horizon, Cody just kept on pulling and we did a big old roll to the right. "That's called a barrel roll, Eddie," Cody said. "How are you doing?"

"Really good," I screamed, suddenly finding my voice. This is neat."

Cody maneuvered all over the place on the way back. I couldn't believe how much fun it was to play around in the sky. That's the only thing I could think of that described my feelings—playing. It was kind of scary in a way, but it was fun too.

Cody interrupted my thoughts. "We're going to land now, Eddie. We're getting low on gas. I'll be making a big old lazy right turn now until I line up with the runway. Can you see it?"

"I can see it, Cody. Boy, it looks pretty small from here." I watched as he just kept turning and inching the airplane down toward the ground until he arrived right over the end of the runway. When we touched down, the wheels kind of squeaked. "That was the most fun I ever had, Cody, thanks a lot."

As he taxied in I looked at my hands. They were all sweaty. So was my chin and most everything else. I guess flying acrobatics made you nervous the very first time. Cody suddenly gunned the engine and whipped the aircraft around to it's parking place. He shut the engine down as soon as we hit our spot.

When I jumped down from the wing, I looked around and saw Dad. He had that proud look on his face. I almost felt like crying, but I didn't. I think it was because I was so happy. Dad shook hands with me and then gave me a big hug. Then, I saw Jack. We ran over and met, just standing there for a minute, looking at each other. Then we danced around like a couple of nuts. We kept it up until we fell down on the ramp and rolled around. For the whole time we just kept talking, trying to tell each other what we did and how good we felt. Finally, we settled down enough to see Dad helping to refuel the plane. Then Luis jumped in the front cockpit and Dad became the crewchief, helping to start the engine and pull the chocks. I think Dad was almost having as much fun as we were.

Luis was up for a little longer than we were before he came back to land, about forty-five minutes. Dad made a quick exchange with Luis, and they raced off. They were only gone for twenty-five minutes. After Cody shut down the engine, he waited for Dad to climb down from the wing, and then they shook hands. I can't remember when I've seen Dad so happy. He and Cody were still talking and making maneuvers with their hands when they came over to Jack and I. Dad put his arms around both of our shoulders, one on each side, and kind of hugged us. We all looked at each other grinning like crazy.

Finally, Cody butted in. "Well, if you fellers are done congratulating yourselves, I've got a little presentation to make. Follow me," he said heading off for his office, really moving out. We ran after him, while Luis buttoned up the plane. When we entered, Cody walked over to his desk and picked up three light blue tee-shirts. "You are now official members of Cody's Lair," he said handing out the shirts. They had a big yellow star embroidered on the pocket with 'Cody's Cowboys' underneath. "Welcome to the club," he said, patting us all on the back, "Wear them proudly, y'all did good today. Now, if you fellers will excuse me, I have to put my little toy away for the night. He pointed at Jack and me, "You two can help me clean her up in the morning," Then he nodded slightly and touched his hat, "Good evening, Gents, it's been a pleasure."

"Thanks, Cody, good-night," we all sang-out as he walked to the door. He turned and touched the brim of his hat again, and then hurried out to the PT-22 where Luis was waiting. Suddenly, Jack whipped off his shirt and donned the new one. We all followed suit.

Then Dad spoke up. "Come on, **Cowboys**, let's go tell Janet what we did." We ran for the car, eager to talk about our experiences.

Then Jack asked, "Is it okay to call my Mom? She'll be excited too."

————————————

"Sure," Dad said. Then he taught us the words (slightly modified) to the Air Force song as we drove home. We got them down pretty good by the time we arrived, and were singing like crazy when we pulled into the carport: *Off we go, into the wild blue yonder, Climbing high into the sun; Here they come zooming to meet our thunder, At'em boys give'er the gun! Down we dive, spouting our flame from under, off with one helluva roar! We live in fame or go down in flame. Hey! Nothing'll stop CODY'S AIR FORCE!*

Mom must have heard us, because she came out to welcome us home. "Are you all nuts?" She said, giving Jack and me a quick hug, saving the big one for Dad. He swung her around in a circle a couple of times. "Wow," she exclaimed. "I wish you guys could fly everyday." Then she noticed our tee-shirts. "Well look at you," she surveyed all of us. Then her smile turned into a questioning look, "Jim, you didn't take them to a bar or something, did you? What are **Cody's Cowboys**?" We all died laughing.

"Cody gives a tee-shirt to everyone who flies in one of his planes," I explained.

She turned to us and gave us her look. "Now I know you're nuts. Well," she said walking in with her arm around Dad's waist, "At least I don't have to cook tonight. You can blame Jim for that, boys. He called earlier and said we were going out to celebrate." She looked at us again, standing there, our faces all smiles. "I think I am going to deserve two Margaritas tonight." Then she looked at Jack and I, composing her thoughts.

"I know, I know," I said, reading her mind, "Go clean up and put on some clean clothes—and don't forget to brush your teeth." I must have really caught her by surprise, because she just stood there laughing, shaking her head. With that, we ran for the bedroom.

Mom hollered after us, "Dad will tell me about his flight first, then you guys will get your chance. Oh, Jack, hold it a minute. I want you to call your Mom. She's waiting to hear what happened. Come with me into my bedroom and we'll call. Eddie, you take your shower now."

"Okay, Mom." Jack put on his brakes and went with Mom. As soon as I got to my bedroom I took off my clothes and headed for the shower. At least I didn't have to flip, I thought, as I turned on the water. Then my mind returned to the skies, which had captured my soul today.

I was dressing when Jack got back. "My Mom was really happy. She said she was real proud of me, too. I know she is, but sometimes I wish I had a dad to help me celebrate important stuff, too," he blurted it out without thinking. "I mean, I like your dad and everything, but it isn't the same as having your own. Know what I mean?" With that, he rushed off to the shower.

"Think about flying," I hollered after him, "That will make you feel better. I'm proud of you, too," I added hoping it might help.

———————————

By the time that Jack was finished cleaning up, everyone was ready to go. Dad was going to take us to Nuevo Laredo, Mexico, to a restaurant called Rincon de Viejo. Mom had everybody's passports, since security had been increased because of the terrorist threat.

"Good thing we learned a little Spanish," Jack said, after we got in the car, "We wouldn't be able to get anything to eat."

"They don't just speak Spanish there do they Dad?" I questioned.

"Oh, most Mexicans can speak enough English so that the majority of American visitors can get by. It is a good idea if you can speak and understand a little bit, though. More than one tourist has ended with something on his plate that he didn't want to eat."

Jack let that soak in for a minute. "Mr. Matthews, what kind of stuff would end up on our plates that we didn't want to eat?"

"Well, Jack, let me see. I guess most of us wouldn't order tripe— that's pig's stomach."

Jack's eyes lit up. "I guess you know what to order, huh Mr. Matthews?'

Dad grinned. "Don't worry, Jack. The place we are going only serves two kinds of meat: cabrito and chicken. You should like either one. They barbecue it over a mesquite wood fire. Either one is excellent. They serve it with soft tortillas, beans, and a salad. They also have Cokes, Water, Cerveza, and Margaritas. The food is really delicious, but the best part is the music. They have a great Mariachi band. I think there are eight musicians. They play different kinds of guitars, trumpets and other horns, and they sing. You're going to love listening to them."

Mom nodded her approval. "They do more than just sing and play. They gather around your table and make you a part of the music. You'll, see. It's so much fun."

It took us a while to get across the bridge and then we had to drive all over the place to find the restaurant. The street was just dirt by the time we found the place. Jack and I were beginning to wonder about Dad's choices in places to eat, although we both liked the last one.

Mom and Dad led the way inside an old adobe wall. We heard singing and music way before we got inside, and the place was pretty noisy when we got to a big wooden deck where there were a bunch of tables with umbrellas sticking out of the middle. There were hardly any electric lights, just strings of little bulbs on wires hanging around. Then I realized, there wasn't any roof—it was outside. All the tables had two or three candles on them which made everything look like what Mom called cozy.

A waiter met us and helped Mom with her chair. Then he took out his pad and took our order. We all decided on Cabrito, which I found out was goat. Mom and Dad said it was good, so Jack and I decided to go along with them. The waiter brought some chips, salsa, and our drinks. Jack and I chowed down right away on the chips and stuff. Mmmm, the salsa was really good. In no time, it seemed, the waiter came back with four plates full of Cabrito, bowls of beans, and a big plate full of tortillas covered with a napkin. Mom got a Margarita, Dad had a Cerveza, and we had Cokes. Boy, they were right, the Cabrito was really good, kind of a cross between chicken and pork—and it had some super spicy sauce. Jack and I filled our tortillas with beans and gulped them down. Well, most of them anyway—some ended up on our shirts.

About half way through our meal we were suddenly surrounded by eight musicians dressed like Mexican Cowboys. They had black outfits: big big hats, long sleeved shirts, and tight pants with silver stars and stuff all up and down their arms and legs. Then they started playing and singing. Mom was right, it was fun. Sometimes one of them would let out kind of a yell—something like eeaah hooo—yip, yip, yip. It was neat. Pretty soon, they had Jack and I yipping with them. Dad gave them some money after they finished. I guess that is how they get paid. Finally, we finished. As usual, Jack and I were stuffed. I guess all of that flying and other adventures we'd been having made us super hungry—again.

It took us longer to get back across the bridge then when we came, but it wasn't too long. We all decided to serenade, Mom, and started singing the Cody Air Force song. By the time we got home, she was singing it too. Some times, Mom could be just as silly as Dad.

We piled out of the car and headed for our room. Andy was already curled up on his bed and barely woke up to see us. I think we were asleep within minutes after we hit the pillows. I started dreaming away about flying. I'll bet Jack probably was too.

———————————

Dad got us up the next morning. Since we were pretty clean, we didn't have to take a shower. After we brushed our teeth and gave our faces a quick splash-off, we jumped into our jeans, new yellow shirts, and headed for the kitchen.

Something smelled awfully good. "Wow! Mom, you made pancakes. Yeah!" Jack and I danced around until Mom made me feed Andy, probably to quiet us down. Then, we both talked a solid stream while Mom cooked, telling her all about our flying experiences, again. She dished up right away, and Jack and I couldn't talk much with all of those pancakes and syrup in our mouths, oh well, she'd heard most of it before. Dad joined us right after we were served and attacked a stack of six pancakes. Boy, could he eat. I wondered if his flight in the PT-22 made him hungrier than usual too.

I remembered something from last night that I wanted to ask Dad. "Hey, Dad. What did you call that restaurant last night? Does it mean anything in English?"

In between bites, he answered. "*Rincon de Viejo*, that means the corner of the old man," he said, taking another mouthful.

"I don't get it," Jack said.

"Me neither," I added.

Dad thought a minute. "I'm not positive, but I think that before it was a restaurant, it was the corner where an old man lived. Before we had maps and addresses, people used to give directions by telling you where things were from a known landmark. In this case, most people probably knew that an old man lived there. Then, for example, they would say: my house is five hundred meters west from the *Rincon de Viejo*. Understand?"

We all nodded, including Mom. Sometimes my Dad could be pretty smart.

"Finally, Dad finished eating. Okay, boys, we'd better get going if you're going to help Cody clean up that toy of his." We shoveled in the last remnants of our pancakes, and headed for the car.

"Don't I get a kiss?" Mom said, as we rushed out the door.

"I'll blow you one," I hollered, sending her a fat juicy one.

"Me too," Jack yelled, blowing her a doozy. "Great breakfast, Mrs. Matthews," he added, never missing a chance to suck up.

Dad caught her and planted a good one right on the lips, catching her by surprise. She was standing there kind of in a trance when we pulled out. Boy, parents are weird.

CHAPTER TEN

We arrived at Cody's Lair about seven-thirty. Luis walked in right after we got there. The PT-22 was near the front, next to the large hanger door. Luis walked to the corner and activated a giant switch. The door started moving toward the side in six foot sections, kind of folding together like cards in a deck. Pretty soon, it was all folded up next to the end. The sun was rising and casting rays of light on the little airplane, making it absolutely beautiful.

Luis wheeled up a small cart filled with bottles, flat tins, and folded up cloths. "This is liquid wax," He picked up a bottle, "You pour some on a cloth and rub in on the aircraft in a circling motion like this," he showed us on a section of the left wingtip. "Then I come along behind you with this electric polisher and shine it up." He held up one of the tins. "This is paste wax. We will only use it on a few sections, I'll show you which ones after we finish with the liquid stuff. There is a small ladder over there you can use for the parts you can't reach from the floor. Well, that's about it. Let's do this wing. We'll get the bottom first, then the top." With that, he plugged in the long chord into an outlet on the hanger floor. "The sooner we get started, the sooner we finish."

"Wow," Jack said to me, "This looks tough. It's going to take us all day, I'll bet."

"No it won't," Luis sung out. "It goes really fast. We should be done in a couple of hours. Remember, we're a good team."

Jack and I got on each side of the wing and started working on the bottom. Before you know it, we had finished the wing. Luis was following us and making the wax shine like everything. We went to the other side and were halfway done by the time Luis finished polishing up the first one. After we finished the bottom of the plane, we started on the top. It was much easier—faster too. We took a break after a little more than one hour, and had a coke. Then we finished up all of the liquid stuff. Luis showed us where to put the paste wax: The walkway on top of the wing, the top of the cowl around the engine, and the prop. There wasn't too much to cover, and it went pretty fast.

By the time Jack and I finished and had washed the gunk off our hands, Luis was done polishing. "Hey, Eddie." Luis hollered, "How about putting some armor-all on the wheels? Jack, you can get the instrument panel and the leather-like stuff around the cockpits, okay?" Thirty minutes later, we were through—two hours on the button. "See," Luis beamed, "I told you we were a good team." We stood back and looked at the little plane. Every little part of it glistened in the morning sun.

"It was worth it, every minute." Jack said, "I'd do it all by myself for another flight."

"Wow," I exclaimed. "Is that coming from you, Jack? The guy that complains his head off about mowing the lawn?" I grabbed him around the shoulder. "I know what you mean, Jack. I think I'd do it by myself, too."

Jack looked at the other planes. "Luis, do you think Cody will take us up in his other two toys?"

Luis smiled. "After he sees the job we did on the PT-22, I think it's a good possibility."

That's just what Jack wanted to hear. He ran over and looked at the other two. "Maybe we can get Cody to tell us about these, Eddie. I'd like to hear their stories, even if we don't get to fly in them."

Luis answered. "Well, guys, whatever is going to happen about these planes, it won't happen for at least a week. We've got a lot of business at Tarantula Field starting Monday. We won't have time to do anything else." He noticed our interest. "Let's go on over to the cafeteria where it's cool, and sit around until they serve lunch. I can give you a run-down on the Tarantula operation, and what you can expect us to do next week." We both nodded our agreement and buttoned up the hanger.

When the big doors clanked to a close, we headed out toward the main base. It was already getting hot—probably going to be in the high nineties, I figured.

———————————

It was ten something when we got to the cafeteria. The smells from breakfast still hung in the air, making Jack hungry. "They don't start serving lunch until eleven-thirty," Luis said. "We can get drinks, though. They got cokes, coffee, milk, tea, and juice. I usually get orange juice, it kind of perks me up after I have been working."

"Boy, Mom would really like you, Luis, you always order healthy stuff. "That does sound good, though. I think I'll get orange juice too."

"Me, too," Jack said, after about an hour of deciding, copying us anyway.

We chose a table over by a window. It was another sunny day. I'm not sure if I'd seen a cloud since we've been here, I was thinking, seeing the heat rise in waves from the cement.

After we had refreshed ourselves a little, Luis started telling us about Tarantula Field. "It all has to do with the Federal requirements to become a pilot—getting a license and stuff. I'll start there, before I tell you what goes on at Tarantula.

Before you get a pilot's license you've got to be sixteen and have a medical certificate saying you aren't sick and your eyes are okay. Before then, like us, you can fly with an approved FAA instructor-pilot, but not by yourself. Once you're sixteen, and the instructor lets you solo, then you can go up by yourself, but can't carry any passengers until you do a bunch of other stuff like making a cross-country flight. You also need to have forty-five hours in your log-book. Once you pass all the tests, both written and flying, the instructor can approve your application for a private pilot's license.

"What's a log-book?" Jack asked.

"It's just a small notebook that you use to keep track of you're flying time, and a couple of other things: what kind of aircraft you flew, the amount of time you actually spent in the air, and sometimes the instructor writes down what maneuvers you have learned. Before you take an airplane up by yourself for the first time, called soloing, the instructor has to write in there that he is letting you do it."

"Can we get a log-book?" I asked.

"Sure. I'll bet your dad has already got a couple for you guys. Don't say anything, but I heard him talking about it with Cody."

"Wow. Our very own log-book," Jack marveled.

"Then what do we do at Tarantula?" I asked, "We're not going to be flying are we?" I said, hoping I was wrong.

Luis finished his juice. "Hold it a minute. Let's get a re-fill. I'm still thirsty." We both nodded and followed Luis over to the beverage bar.

After we returned, and had a good long drink, Luis continued. "Let's see, where shall I start? Okay, I mentioned the requirements to get a license. But then you need to have a place to do all of that takeoff and landing practice. It's hard to do at a regular field because of all of the routine traffic—and student pilots can be dangerous at times because they get in the way of other pilots. So the student pilots have to get their practice at an auxiliary field. Of course, there are all kinds of rules about running an auxiliary field. They come from the FAA, the State of Texas, and from Cody. I'm not sure which one says what, exactly. Anyway, we have to have a fire truck there. They check the runway right after they get there to make sure there isn't anything on it that would be a hazard to a plane. Then, they park on a cement pad somewhere near the middle of the field, so they can rush out and put out a fire if a plane crashes on the runway."

"The next thing that's required is having a control tower. At Tarantula we have an old mobile unit left over from the Air Force. Opening it up is my job. I unlock the unit, turn on the power, and check the radios. I also load the flare pistols, clean off the binoculars, and clean all of the windows once a week. I stay there until the first instructor-pilot is dropped off—each school supplies it's own instructor. I also make sure the privy's are clean and that the refrigerator is well stocked with coke and other pop—a delivery man or the fire crew brings drinks out there once a month. Then, after flying is over, I put everything back and lock up and go home."

"You said you flew out there with Cody, and then he picked you up." I reminded him.

He nodded. "Sometimes. If I'm going to be out there all day, I normally ride out with the fire crew. But most of the time, we are only busy for a few hours. Then I go with Cody. It all depends upon what the flying schools schedule, or what comes up at the last minute. Once in a while Cody acts as the instructor for Lone Star—that's when I get to fly."

That triggered a question from Jack. "What do you do after the instructors get there? Do you just sit there with them and watch? It must get pretty boring being by yourself."

Luis nodded again. "Yep. That's why I'm so happy you guys are here. It does get pretty monotonous messing around out there all by yourself. Once in a while something neat happens, like finding Porky, but it's usually a drag." He continued, "Of course, we can watch the spiders and stuff together. You'll like that."

Then Jack noticed that the food line was getting ready to open. "Come on, you guys, let's go get a hamburger."

———————————

After lunch, we headed back to Cody's office to see if he had anything for us to do. He said a customer had just dropped off a Piper, at hanger two, that needed to be cleaned up. We decided that we could get the task done before we had to leave, so we eagerly took on the job.

It only took us a little over an hour to wash the airplane, and we happily proceeded back to the office to see if there was anything else he wanted us to do. There wasn't, so we just sat down and talked about our day.

Pretty soon, Dad showed up and took Jack and I home. We had the weekend off, and planned to mess around the house. We'd asked

Luis if he could come over for dinner on Sunday, and he'd accepted. It would be a quiet weekend, but we deserved a little rest, after all, we'd been working our tails off, and been busy having adventures. So far, it had been a pretty good summer.

———————————

When we pulled into the carport, Dad pointed out that the lawn needed mowing. "You two can get it done before dinner if you hurry," he suggested.

"Awww, Dad. We already washed a plane this afternoon, and I need to play with Andy—I've hardly seen him all week—and I have to feed him, too." I was thinking of even more stuff I needed to do when he relented.

"Okay. But I want it done first thing in the morning. "Actually, it will be cooler then, I guess. But don't forget." He walked toward the bedroom to change.

"Boy, that was a close one," Jack said, as we walked outside. "I guess it doesn't look too bad. We should be able to knock it out in an hour or so. It's too hot now, we would melt if we went out there to work."

I played with Andy for a while, until both of us got too hot. I went over and checked the thermometer that was hanging in the carport. I hollered at Jack, who was sitting in the shade of the porch, "Wow, Jack, it's one hundred and one out here. No wonder we're hot. Let's go see if we can talk Mom out of a coke or something."

I got Andy's water dish and filled it up with fresh water. "Mom, did you know it's one hundred and one out there? Jack and I are dying of thirst. Can we have a coke?"

She looked up from the counter where she was getting stuff ready for dinner. "No, but you can have some juice—it will replace the fluid you lost better than coke. There's apple and orange, take your pick."

"How about apple?" I said to Jack, who was standing behind me.

He shrugged. "Why not?"

We put some ice in our glasses and filled them with apple juice. Actually, it was pretty thirst quenching. We sat in the shade of the porch to take a rest. Then the sun got behind a big tree next to the carport, and it really cooled off. I Guess the humidity wasn't very high. Andy was curled up at our feet catching a quick before-dinner nap.

Dad walked back into the kitchen and started talking with Mom. "Can I give you a hand with anything Honey?"

"I guess you could smush this garlic in with the butter over there on the counter, and then spread it on the bread. Then you can wrap it in aluminum foil."

"You bet, Sweetheart. I love garlic-bread with spaghetti. Are you making a salad too?"

"Yes, I'm making your favorite. The one with feta cheese."

Dad's eyes lit up with that remark. "How long before we eat?"

Mom checked her watch. "I haven't started the pasta yet. It will probably be ready in a half hour. I guess we can sit down about six-thirty. By the way, how are things going out at work? You haven't said much about it lately."

Dad pulled up a chair at the kitchen table, and started smushing garlic. "Not so hot, Honey. We are bringing in another plane so that we can increase our surveillance time."

"Really. Haven't you been able to pin-point anything with the Gulfstream so far?"

Dad shook his head. "Not a thing. It's a mystery. We can see trucks driving down the highways in Mexico, but we can't seem to spot whatever they are using to get these terrorists across the border. Did I tell you the FBI arrested another guy in Ft.Worth?"

Mom, stopped working and turned to Dad. "No, you didn't. Golly, Jim. Are you sure they are coming in from Mexico?"

"We're never completely sure. This guy apparently admitted entering Mexico through Tampico, on an old steamer—but we haven't a clue how he got up north. The next thing we knew is that he is running around Ft. Worth with all kinds of false documents, close to a million in cash, and plans of the DFW airport. He had to get across the border somewhere. We are watching the coastline and border all the way from New Orleans to California—and I mean we are checking everything we see. So far, we have produced nothing tangible."

"That's a big area, Jim. You can't expect to see everything, can you?"

He slapped the table. "I guess we can't spot every little item that crosses over the border, but we should be able to spot people carrying suitcases full of materials. It's really frustrating. We have a team checking out the electronic ground security equipment along the river, and it all seems to be functioning without a problem. The guy told me that his stuff is so good they can track groups of Javelina running around. Lord, if they can do that, you would think they could track a couple of people, carrying bags of money and stuff."

"Well, what are you going to do?"

"For now, we're going to increase our flying time. That will allow us to check on anything that the ground equipment is picking up. Maybe together, we can figure out what they are doing."

I walked into the kitchen. "Mom. When are we going to eat? Oh, Boy. Mmmm. You're making spaghetti."

"Yes, we're having spaghetti. We should be ready to sit down in about fifteen minutes. How about you and Jack going in and washing up. Has Andy been fed?"

"Yeah. I fed him a little while ago. We don't have to shower do we? We're just going to get filthy dirty doing the lawn early tomorrow morning."

Mom looked at Dad—who winked. "I guess not. But run out and check the mail before you wash your face and hands."

"Yes, Mom." I ran out and got the mail, and tossed it on the living-room table, then joined Jack in the bathroom. We washed up and changed shirts, just in case Mom noticed the gunk we had gotten on them from washing the airplane.

We were walking toward the kitchen when Mom handed me a letter. "It's from Victoria, she said, giving me that silly little wink.

I looked at it quickly. Sure enough, it was from Victoria. I went out to the back porch to get a little privacy, then opened the letter. She said she was coming to Laredo with her aunt on the fifteenth, and would be here for about—What! Three weeks. What in the world were we going to do with her for three whole weeks—just when Jack and I were really starting to have some fun. When is the fifteenth? Let's see, today is the ninth—Oh no, that's only six days from now. What was I going to tell Jack?

"Eddie. Dinner's on," Mom hollered from the kitchen.

I went into the dining room and joined everybody at the table. We had hardly finished saying Grace when Mom started grilling me. "Is Victoria coming for a visit?" she started.

"Uh huh," I said, "Pass the bread please."

"Victoria's coming?" Jack said, looking surprised. "When?"

Everyone at the table was staring at me, waiting for my answer. It took a minute for me to swallow. "On the fifteenth," I answered, almost choking. I could see Jack's brain trying to figure out how much freedom we had left. "Six days from now," I said, and she's going to be here for three whole weeks."

"That's almost the rest of the summer," Jack protested. "What are we going to do with her?" he blurted out without remembering he was in front of Mom.

"You won't have to **do** anything with her," Mom answered, curtly. "But I think out of common courtesy you would want to show her around a little. Poor thing, she will be all by herself all day while her aunt teaches. The least you can do is volunteer to do a few things together. Couldn't she help you with the planes? I'll bet she will be fascinated with the things you two have learned about flying, too." I just kept on nodding while Jack kept his eyes on his plate—he didn't want to be included.

Dad had a big grin on his face, knowing what we were up against, but he didn't come to our defense—the chicken. Then, finally, he spoke. "Come on, you guys. It's not that big a deal. You can show her the planes and stuff. I'm sure she will get bored with the whole thing pretty quick. I doubt if a girl would be interested in washing airplanes or going out to Tarantula Field. Those things are too hot and dirty for a girl."

Mom gave Dad one of her looks. Oh. Oh. Here it comes, I thought. "Girls do <u>so</u> like to do that kind of thing. They don't just sit around and read, take piano lessons, and knit. <u>Not anymore!</u>"

"Oh, Janet. You know I didn't mean that. I just think it's awfully hot and dusty out in the open, and there aren't any facilities or anything for girls in some of those places."

"There weren't any facilities on the Oregon Trail, or at the Alamo, either. But that didn't stop strong women from being there—doing their part." Dad knew when he was licked, so he just took another helping and ate.

It was getting awful quiet, so I spoke up. "Heck, Mom. I didn't say we wouldn't take her anywhere. I'm sure we can fine something that she likes to do. She wasn't so bad on that project we did. Maybe she will be able to fit in here too."

Mom's eyes lit up. "Now that's the spirit. I'm glad to see we have at least one member of this family with some common sense. More bread, anyone?" We all stuck up our hands.

After dinner, while drying the dishes, I asked Mom what she was going to have for Luis, when he came over on Sunday. "Can you cook Mexican food? I asked.

She looked at me kind of funny. "No, Eddie. I can't cook Mexican food like they do here in Laredo." She hesitated for a moment, then continued. "Just because someone has a certain ethnic background, like Luis, who comes from a Mexican family, it doesn't mean that they only do or like what comes from their heritage. Luis is an American. He also has a Mexican heritage. That doesn't mean that he has to choose from which culture he belongs to. He can do the same as us. My parents family came from Germany. Dad's parents were primarily English. That doesn't mean we have to just do what is English or German. We are Americans, we can choose what we want to be and what cultures we want to emulate. I'm sure he loves Mexican food—so do I, but that doesn't mean we have to serve it when he comes here for dinner."

I thought about what she said for a minute. "Gee, Mom, I never thought about it that way. I mean, I wouldn't want him to feel like he wasn't an American. I just thought that he was probably used to eating

Mexican food and we ought to make him feel at home. I guess I never thought that he would like ham or something like that."

She gave me a big hug. "I understand exactly what you mean, Eddie. I know you were thinking that we ought to do something special to make him feel comfortable when he comes to our house. But the way to make someone to feel comfortable, is to treat them just like one of the family. Do you understand?"

"Sure, but you aren't going to make him help dry the dishes or anything are you?"

She grabbed me and gave me a big hug. "Of course not. Unless he wants to help. That might be just the thing that would make him feel at home." She laughed, and kind of cuffed me on the head. "Thanks for helping me, Eddie, I think you are growing up to be a pretty neat boy." She had a tear in her eye when I left. Sometimes Mom's can be pretty neat themselves.

After leaving the kitchen, I joined Jack in our bedroom. We talked a little about Victoria coming, but neither of us worried about it much. I think that Jack thought she was okay, and wouldn't cause us any trouble—me too—we just didn't want to admit it to grown ups.

Later we turned in, wanting to be rested before doing the lawn in the morning. I moved Andy to his pillow, and, to my surprise, he didn't hardly Grrr me at all. It had been a long day and we all quickly dropped off to sleep.

Jack and I were up early the next morning and mowed the lawn. Afterwards, Mom made us clean up, because she insisted that we had to go to the mall with her to buy some new clothes. She wanted us to look nice for Victoria.

I suppose we didn't look too happy when we got in the car. "Oh, come on, you guys. You need some new khakis and a couple of polo shirts. It's not going to be that bad," Mom said, driving towards town. "You just can't wear those old raggedy jeans everywhere, you need something a little nicer." We knew better than to argue with Mom once she had her mind made up, so we decided to agree with what ever she liked. Then, we could get it over with quickly, without having to try on everything in the store.

The store was pretty nice. We went to the Young Man's Department, and were greeted by a guy in a suit. He suggested several outfits, but Mom just kept on looking. Then she spotted some pants she liked, and matched them with a couple of polo shirts. Actually, they didn't look bad. At least they weren't pink or some other dumb color that a girl would wear. The salesman measured our waists and inseam and picked out the right size. Of course, we had to try them on anyway. When we came out of the dressing room, Mom looked surprised. "Well, what do you know. Eddie, remember when we talked about growth spurts?" I nodded yes. How could I forget that day? "Well, it looks like you two have grown. I think these pants are two inches longer than your others.

Then it sunk in. "Does that mean I'm two inches taller?"

She nodded. "You too, Jack. I think you have both grown a couple of inches in the last few months."

Jack looked proud. "When can we get measured to know for sure?" he asked.

The salesman interrupted. "Excuse me, we can do that right over here. We have a tape on the wall." He stood us up with our backs to the wall and put a little carpenters square over our heads. "Let's see. Eddie, is it? You are exactly sixty-three inches." He measured Jack. "And you are exactly sixty-two inches." Jack looked disheartened.

I slugged him. "Hey, Jack, you gained an inch on me. I used to be two inches taller than you, remember?" That cheered him up a bit, but not entirely. He walked back over to the wall and held the square over his head and checked the height.

"Nuts, I'm still sixty-two inches," he said, still dejected.

Then Mom piped up. "Won't Victoria be surprised when she sees you two. She'll notice how much taller you both are."

I got to thinking about that. I wondered if girls had growth spurts, too. Then I decided that in either case I was probably gaining on her. At least her mom wasn't very tall, that was good news.

After we got home, Jack and I messed around for a while, and generally got bored. "I'd rather be having an adventure," Jack said, kicking some dirt in Oscar's hole. "Why don't we wander around the neighborhood?" We took a walk and didn't find much—just houses.

The next morning, after Church, Mom made Jack write a letter to his mom while I played around with Andy. After that, I dried a few glasses and dishes for Mom. Then I noticed our good dishes on the counter. "Why are you using your good stuff?" I asked her, "You normally don't use these plates except at Thanksgiving and Christmas."

She was humming a little tune while she worked. "Well, first of all, I like them—don't you? Secondly, I want Luis to know that we think he is special."

I helped Mom carry the dishes to the table a gave her a hand putting them out. "The dishes are kind of pretty, I guess. I do like the way they look. The glasses are pretty too, except I'm always afraid I'll knock one over and break the stem off. Luis might worry about that, too. I'm not sure if I would feel special if I was worried about breaking something the whole time

I was eating."

"Well, I think he will feel just fine." She kept humming away as she checked everything out. Satisfied, she walked back in the kitchen.

"What are we having for dinner?"

"Roast beef, mashed potatoes and gravy, and string beans. Plus a special dessert."

I was starting to get hungry just hearing about it. "What time are we eating? Luis said he would be here about three o'clock."

"I wanted him to get here about an hour early, so we'll eat about four."

"Is Dad going to go get him?"

"No. He's going to ride his bike. He and his mom only live about five blocks away."

I must have looked surprised. "I wonder how he gets to the base. I've seen a bike out there, but I didn't think that he rode it all the way from home."

"He might ride with his mom. She works out there, doesn't she?"

That must be it, I figured. I had forgotten that his mom worked out there too. "I'll ask him when he gets here," I said, "If he rides his bike, then maybe Jack and I could ride with him sometimes. Jack and I both love to ride bikes. Then Dad wouldn't have to take us all the time."

Mom looked a little worried at that one. "I'm not sure about that, but I'll ask Jim to look into it." She went on getting everything ready, still humming, when I left to checkout what Jack was doing.

————————————

Luis knocked on the door at three o'clock on the dot. He looked pretty nice, he had on almost the same outfit as us. I guess all moms must look at clothes the same way, I was thinking as I introduced him to Mom. "Luis, this is my Mom. Mom, this is Luis Rodriguez."

They shook hands. "It's nice to meet you Luis, the boys have told me a lot about you," she said smiling.

He smiled back. "I have known you're husband for quite a while now," he said, "So I'm happy to finally meet you. Welcome to Laredo." He gave her a small gift, then gave a quick look at Jack and me. "I hope what the boys said about me wasn't all bad," he joked.

"Of course not, Luis," Mom, said as she was opening the package. "All they told me was the good stuff." She winked. "Oh, Luis," Mom said as she held up a small silver book-mark. "What a lovely gift." She gave him a big hug. "I love to read, and I will always think of you when I use it. Thank you so much, Luis."

Just then Dad came in and gave Luis a second welcome. Mom said we weren't going to eat for a while, so Jack and I took him outside to meet Andy. Mom had stuck him out back so he wouldn't bark and jump-up while everybody was saying hello. Andy came over and gave him a quick sniff, then jumped up and barked his greeting. Luis gave him a quick scratch on the head, which turned into a tummy-rub, naturally. We messed around out back and showed Luis the hole where Oscar the Armadillo lived. He knew all about Armadillos and told us a lot of stuff they didn't cover in my nature book.

Pretty soon it was time for dinner. Mom told us to wash up, so we all ran in and rinsed off our hands. Mom showed Luis where to sit and Dad led the Grace. Luis joined in and said the whole thing perfect. He even made a little cross with his hand over his forehead and chest after we finished. Mom served up, and didn't even have to tell Luis to wait until everybody got a plate. He had good manners, too, and used all of the right silverware—like using a second fork for his salad. He ate all of his vegetables, too. Mom gave him an admiring glance. I knew she was going to love him ever since I saw him order orange juice instead of coke at the restaurant.

Mom started clearing the table when we had finished eating the main dinner. "Luis, where do you go to school? Is there a good one nearby?"

"I go to St. Mary's, Mrs. Matthews. It's only about six blocks from here. Cody got me started there. He said it was the best school in town and thought that the Nuns would keep me in line. He was right on both counts," he grinned. "We have a pretty modern school, too. We have a neat science laboratory, and a brand new computer center. We even get lap-tops to take home if we need them for some project or other. It's also the best place for non-Spanish speakers to learn the language—they call it total imersion. Anyway, most everyone learns to speak the language after being there for only one year."

Mom's eyes lit up. "What a wonderful opportunity for Eddie, Jim. Do you think we could get him enrolled there?"

Dad nodded. "Let me check with Cody to get the lay of the land, first, before we approach them. "Luis, do they have any non-Catholic kids there?"

"Sure, Mr. Matthews. Quite a few. A lot of my friends aren't Catholic."

Then, Mom popped up. "How would you boys like some strawberry shortcake?" We all threw up our hands, including Dad. Mom disappeared for a minute and came back with two heaping plates of strawberry shortcake, covered with a big mound of whip-cream. We all looked at each other, trying not to lick our chops or something. It was hard to wait until everyone was served, but we managed.

"Mmmm. There's nothing better than this," I said, wiping a big glob of whip-cream off my nose. Everybody mumbled their agreement, nodded their heads, and just kept eating.

After dinner, we sat around and talked a little while in the living room, until Luis had to go. He thanked Mom and Dad, and then reminded us that we needed to make sandwiches for our trip to Tarantula Field on Monday. We all waved good-bye as he headed off up the street on his bike. "I think he did have a good time, Mom," I said, "And I think he did appreciate the good china and crystal—he didn't have any trouble at all."

She gave me a little one armed hug as we went inside. "Why don't you and Jack go in your room and take it easy, listen to some music or something. I'll get Jim to help with the dishes." With that I ran for it before she could change her mind. "I'll make two sandwiches for each of you," she hollered, "and an apple, too."

Jack and I piled on our bunks and just relaxed—full as ticks. Andy joined us and jumped on his pillow. It had been a great day.

CHAPTER ELEVEN

We woke up at first light. It was a little after six. We both dressed and put on our hiking boots. Mother insisted upon us wearing them because there might be snakes out at the auxiliary field. We had cereal and toast for breakfast while Mom made us two sandwiches each—peanut butter and jam, and lunchmeat and cheese. She also put an apple in each of our sacks. "Are you sure you will have something to drink out there? I can fix you a thermos of juice."

"No, Mom," I said, finishing up my toast. "Luis said there is plenty of water and lots of different kinds of pop." She looked a little worried, but relented. "Besides, we can't carry a big old thermos on our bikes," I added, to make her understand better.

"I don't want you two over doing it today at Tarantula Field. If you are too tired to ride your bikes home this afternoon from the Base, just call. I'll come pick you up."

"Yes, Mom," I said, and Jack nodded as we left through the carport door. "Let's go, if you want to get there before the fire truck leaves. You ride about as fast as a snail."

Jack quickly passed me. "Oh, yeah, I'm Lance Armstrong—try and catch me."

He raced ahead for about a block before he wore down a little and I passed him back.

"You sure aren't Lance Armstrong," I hollered, as I whizzed by. "He can go five times faster than this all the way around France. You can hardly make it for two blocks."

"I'm just saving my energy like your mom told us," he said, puffing away. "I want to be ready to do extra stuff out there at Tarantula."

That made sense, I decided, and slowed down a bit. No sense wearing myself out just to beat Jack. Heck, I've ridden a bike for my whole life, and Tarantula would be a whole new ballgame—and I needed to be fresh in case something really neat happens. "Okay, Jack, but we had better keep going pretty fast. I don't want to be late."

We got to the base with no problems. There was hardly any traffic until we got to Highway, 59, out front of the base. We walked our bikes across the highway, and then peddled over to Cody's office. Luis was already there. His mom had dropped him off, along with a little dog-crate with Porky inside. I'd almost forgotten that we were going to turn his Javelina loose today. He was as mean as ever, squealing and snorting away. "Hi, Luis," I said, "Morning Porky." I turned to Luis, "Do we need to do anything before we go?"

Luis shook his head and shrugged, "Can't think of anything. We just have to wait here until the fire truck comes by."

"Here they come," Jack hollered, pointing down the flightline. "Luis, do they always drive with their lights on?"

Luis looked up. "Yes, now that you mentioned it. I don't know why. Probably has something to do with being on the flightline area." We nodded our agreement, made sense to us.

It didn't take us long to get loaded up and were soon speeding toward the Tarantula Field turnoff, about thirty miles from the base. The auxiliary field was about two miles from the highway, and was connected by an old dusty road. We bounced along about fifteen miles per hour and finally got there. The driver didn't stop; he just took off down the right side of the runway until we got to the north end. Then he turned around and came back along the other side, to where the tower and other buildings were located. We unloaded our stuff, along with a couple of cases of pop and bottled water—and Porky, of course. As soon as we had everything cleared away, the truck went back and parked on a pad about half-way down the runway.

"Let's open up the mobile tower first," Luis said, sorting through a big ring of keys. "Here's the one." He unlocked the door and we went inside. It wasn't very big; the floor was about six foot square. "This is the refrigerator," Luis pointed to a small under-counter unit. "You can fill it up, Eddie, and then we'll put the rest in another fridge in that building over there. It will hold eight of each kind."

I looked inside. "Jack, I think we can use seven Cokes, two Orange Crush, four Dr. Peppers, and six waters."

Jack started sorting out the bottles and cans. "Here's the Cokes and Orange," he said, re-checking how many Dr. Peppers we needed. "Oh, yeah, four," he remembered. He brought the cans to me while I stocked the shelves. "What now? Luis," Jack asked.

"Why don't you just watch me," he said. "First, I'll show you how to turn on the radios. This is the master switch. Turn it on first. There, see that light? That means we have ground power. If that light didn't come on, it means you have to go and crank up that big old emergency generator over there. I'll show you how to do that later. Then you turn on the function switch, here." Another green light came on. He picked up one of two microphones lying on the counter. "Laredo tower, this is Tarantula for a radio check. How do you read, over?"

There was a crackling noise. "Roger, Tarantula, I read you five by five. How me, over."

"I read you five square, Laredo. Have you got any traffic for us yet?"

"There is a one seventy-two headed your way with a couple of instructors on board. They should check in pretty soon."

"Thanks, Laredo, Tarantula out." He pointed to another switch. "This is where I turn on the monitor for the weather information. See." He clicked the switch, and a bunch of dials and needles moved. "These are the wind direction and speed, and this is the current altimeter setting."

Jack spoke up. "Wow, Luis. That's neat. Who taught you to how to talk on the radio and all this other stuff?"

"Cody did. Don't worry, you'll learn," he said, while he turned on the air conditioner. "It's easy after you do it yourself once or twice and listen for a while. And Cody will probably loan you his walkie-talkies. He's got three or four of them. You can practice with each other while you are out messing around. It helps."

"Hey, Eddie, maybe we can get Victoria to help us learn. She's real good at languages and stuff. I'll bet she could pick up the radio language in no time."

"Who's Victoria?" Luis asked.

Jack answered. "She's our friend from Homestead."

Luis started nodding his head. "Oh, yeah, I remember. That's Virginia Porter's niece. You said she might come for a visit."

"Yeah, she's coming next week," Jack answered. "We call her the brain at school, because she's so smart."

I jumped in the conversation. "She's not that smart. But I guess she's smart enough to learn radio talk like Jack said."

We were both interrupted by a call on the radio. "Tarantula tower, this is Cessna two niner six, three miles southeast for landing."

Luis grabbed the mike. "Roger two niner six, you are cleared for landing runway three zero zero. Winds zero one five at four knots. Altimeter, two niner niner eight. The runway is clear, crash-rescues in place."

154

"Roger, Tarantula. See you in a minute." We looked to the south and saw a small silver airplane headed our way. A couple of minutes later it landed right in front of us, turned around about halfway down the runway, and taxied back. Then they turned off onto a small apron next to the mobile unit.

Luis quickly opened a drawer and pulled out two funny looking guns. "These are Vary-Pistols. They shoot these flares." He picked up what looked like an overgrown shotgun shell and stuck it in the back of one. Then he repeated the process. "One flare is red and the other is green—the same as the handles are painted. The red means danger, stop the landing and take it around. The green means we have lost radios but things are safe." He stuck them in color coded tubes sticking down from the ceiling. Then he reached in another drawer and took out a big set of binoculars. He pulled the caps off of the lenses and gave them a quick wipe with a cloth from the case. "That's all for now. We might need to clean the windows later."

He hopped up and led us out the door. "Come on, I want you to meet these guys. "Hi Tony, I want you to meet a couple of my friends. This is Jack Davis, and this is Eddie Matthews."

Tony was a short guy with bright red hair. He offered his hand. "Tony Flanigan, guys, glad to meet you. I see Luis is teaching you the ropes. Are you going to be pilots too?"

We nodded. "Hi, Mr. Flanigan," I said, shaking hands, "Yes, we'd love to become pilots."

Jack butted in and offered his hand to Tony. "Eddies dad is already a pilot, but I don't have anyone in my family that has flying experience, is it going to be harder for me?"

"Don't worry, Jack. You don't become a better pilot because your dad knows how to fly. You have to work at it all by yourself. It's not as easy as it seems, so just hang in there—and don't be afraid to ask questions." He looked away. "Hey, Luis, do you know Stu Miller?"

Luis turned around and looked at the fellow behind Tony. "Sure. Hi, Stu. Haven't seen you for a while. Have you met my buddies?" We all met and shook hands.

Luis scratched his head. "Why are you both here? You got a solo student coming in here for his cross-country or something, Stu?"

Stu nodded, and then grinned. "I always give them a challenge. I like to use Tarantula, because a weak pilot might to try to land at Laredo. The last kid I soloed made that mistake, and I had to wash him out. You don't belong in this business if you can't tell the difference between a major airfield with two runways, and a little single strip out in the middle of nowhere."

"I think you do that on purpose, Stu," Tony laughed. "I think that's how you get rid of your weak students. Wish I'd have thought of it first," he chuckled. "Which one is coming today, a good one or a bad one?"

"A good one I hope. This kid is a real natural pilot, but, as you know, physical ability's not enough. I need to know if a pilot can think before they are on their own out there with a passenger."

Luis waved. "Sorry to interrupt, but I think Bill is trying to get back in the air. What does he need to do, work on landings?"

"Yeah," Tony answered. "Nice kid but he's got poor depth perception. Probably won't make it, but Bill wanted to give him another shot."

Luis interjected. "Okay, you guys, everything is set up. Tony, would you mind checking out one of the flare guns after Bill's student gets airborne? My buddies have never seen one."

"Sure," Tony answered. "I'll give you a green one." Then he hollered as he was getting into the unit. "Hey, Luis. If it starts a fire, it's your fault." Luis grinned and nodded okay, secretly having his fingers crossed.

As soon as the Cessna took off, Tony fired the flare. "Wow! Neat," Jack exclaimed, looking at me. I agreed, nodding that it was pretty neat. It must have gone up a million feet before it arched over and fell to the ground. It was much neater than fireworks—well, maybe not neater, just different.

Afterwards, we watched the Cessna make landings—try to make landings, I should have said. Poor guy, he looked good until he got within fifty feet of the ground. Then, he bounced all over the place. I guess he couldn't judge the distance to the ground.

We decided he wasn't going to get any better, so we left to let Porky loose. We took our sandwiches and a bottle of water with us. Boy, Porky was a mean little bugger for his size, and he hated that box. Luis carried him past the north end of the runway and finally stopped at the side of an arroyo, a dry river bed, where he'd found him wandering around hungry. He was sure different now, healthy as a regular hog, and spent the whole time raising cane, snorting and squealing. Luis opened his cage and Porky cautiously ventured out. He looked around for a minute or two and then started smelling like mad. I wondered if he smelled other Javelina. Pretty soon he took off a mile a minute, up the arroyo, the way the wind was coming from. We heard other squeals from up there. We all tensed up, hoping that Porky would fit in. We sneaked up and looked over a little bank. There was Porky with a bunch of Javelina. They were all smelling each other and making all kinds of noise. I guessed they recognized him. Cody was right when he said we had needed to get him back before he'd lost what was planted in him—in this case, it was a smell.

Luis made us get out of there before we spooked the Javelina. We wandered down the arroyo for a while, eating our sandwiches, seeing if we could spot a snake or a spider. We weren't successful. Luis kicked a couple of rocks, trying to surprise a couple of spiders. "The tarantulas like it hot, I think. Anyway, I see them mainly in the afternoon. Why don't we go back and I'll show you the rest of the buildings. Then we can see if Stu Miller's student finds the field."

"Boy, those instructors sure make it hard on the students," Jack said. "I guess they can't just let someone have a license unless they prove they can really fly. Sure not like getting a drivers license. I've heard that all you have to do is pass an easy test and drive around the block." We all nodded, knowingly, although none of us had done it.

Luis unlocked the door to the main building where the refrigerator was. We loaded it up, and then Luis picked up the money-can. "Guess I'll see how much we got in here. Huh, that's funny. All of the money is gone except for a few pennies. I'll check with the fire crew. Sometimes they take out enough to replenish the supplies, but they never take all of the change."

"Hey, Luis," Jack hollered. "This window over here is broken."

We all went over to take a look. "Looks like someone threw that big rock through the top part of the window and then reached in and opened the lock." I looked out the window and saw foot prints on the dirt. "Someone was here, all-right."

Luis was shaking his head. "I can't believe it. Who would want to come way out here?" Then he kind of pinched up his lips, and then nodded agreement with himself. "I think some wet-back made it over the river and is headed north—probably needed water for the trip. Wow, that's the first time we've had anything like this. Oh, well, nobody got hurt. Cody will be madder than a hornet though. He really believes in trusting people. He'll say that this guy could have just helped himself to the water, but he shouldn't have stolen the money." We all agreed it was a pretty crummy thing to do.

Then I got to thinking. "Luis, you called him a wet-back. Your folks came up here from Mexico; did people call them wet-backs? Mom says that isn't a very nice term."

"No, they called my folks illegals, now that you mention it. I guess it was because they walked across the bridge instead of wading across the river. I never thought about it much. Maybe they had fake papers," he shrugged. "All I can say is everybody I know calls the people that sneak across the border wet-backs—Mexicans included. Your mom's right, though, it isn't very complimentary, it's just something you get used to hearing living in a border town.

Then Luis took us over to the smaller building about fifty yards to the west. He unlocked the door and we walked in to take a look. "This place is just for storage. We never keep much in here—just extra supplies, emergency equipment, and stuff. Ah, oh, another broken window." It was broken the same way.

"Look, footprints," Jack hollered. Sure enough, there were dirty tracks leading over to a door. "What's in there, Luis?" Jack said kind of scared.

Luis answered. "It's just an old office, nothing in there." He opened the door and we all looked in. There on the floor were a couple of empty water bottles and an old wadded up blanket. "Looks like our burglar slept here. Everything else looks okay. I was right; he probably sneaked across the border and doesn't want to get caught by anybody."

I kind of poked around the blanket and saw a wadded-up dirty old paper laying there. "What's that?" Jack asked.

I took a quick look. "Nothing much. Just some wadded-up old letter or something with some scribbley writing." I tossed it in an old trash can in the corner, along with the two empty plastic water bottles he'd emptied.

Luis checked his watch. "Stu Miller said his student should be here about one o'clock, five minutes from now. Let's go watch him land."

By the time we reached the mobile unit, we heard an aircraft engine. Pretty soon, there was a crackle on the radio. "Tarantula tower, this is Cessna three seven two, request landing instructions." The pilot's voice sounded a little high, but I decided his voice hadn't fully changed yet.

Stu jumped up, really looking proud. "Did you hear that?" he slugged his hand with his fist, "Sounds like an old pro instead of a sixteen year old kid." He grabbed the mike. "Roger, Cessna three seven two, cleared to land runway three zero zero, winds three six zero at five knots, altimeter two niner niner two, call one mile on final."

"Roger, Tarantula. Copy."

Pretty soon, there he was. "Tarantula, Cessna three seven two one mile final, requesting full stop and taxi-back."

Stu smiled. "Roger, we have you in sight, cleared to land." The plane bounced around a little bit as it got close to the ground, but made a real smooth touchdown right in front of us. "All-right," Stu said, giving Tony a high five. "Cessna three seven two, cleared taxi-back when able, park the aircraft on the pad just north of the mobile." He watched a minute until the Cessna made its turn and started back. Stu picked up the mike again, "You done good, Kelli. Bring your log-book with you. I need to sign it. You've earned your license today."

The little Cessna 150 made a sweeping turn-about and parked right next to the mobile. After the engine quit, the pilot got out of the other side and walked around the tail of the aircraft. Then I realized it wasn't a guy at all, it was a girl. She had long blond hair, neat mirrored sunglasses, and had on Levi's and a Polo shirt—even flying gloves. She was all smiles when she approached the unit. Stu went out to meet her. She grabbed him and gave him a big hug, and then she kind of danced around pumping her fist. "Wow!" I said, looking at Jack and Luis. They were as surprised as I was.

We all met Kelli, and then she and Stu hopped in the Cessna and headed for home. It was kind of neat meeting someone who just got their pilot's license, even if it was a girl.

Right after they left, three more planes showed up and made a million touch and go landing. They were better than the guy with the depth perception problems, but not much.

Finally, one of the airplanes made a full stop and parked next to the mobile unit. "Well, guys," Tony said. "Here's my ride. Nice meeting you Eddie—Jack. Luis, it's always a pleasure. Say hello to Cody for me." With that, Tony hopped in the backseat of the Cessna 172, and they departed.

Luis unloaded the flares and put away the binoculars while we dusted things off and swept the floor. It only took us a few minutes. Then Luis let me call Laredo tower to sign out. He wrote everything down for me so I wouldn't screw it up. It was really fun talking on the radio like a real pilot. After turning off the power and locking up, we walked over and re-checked the two buildings, making sure we didn't leave any lights on. By then, Luis had figured out that the burglar had taken forty-eight dollars and eighty cents—bummer. We put cardboard and tape over the broken windows. That would have to do until a repair crew could fix it for good. Then we walked down to the fire-truck and climbed on board. Forty minutes later Jack and I were on our way home from the base, not pumping the peddles quite as hard as we had that morning. Guess we were pretty tired from spending most of the day at Tarantula.

———————————

We filled in Mom about our day, and I went to feed Andy while Jack took a shower. I guess we both must be growing up a little, because I didn't slug Jack, and he didn't even mention flipping.

After dinner that night I told Dad about the burglar. He seemed pretty worried about it, especially if Luis's theory about him entering illegally was true. It made him wonder if there might be something wrong with the ground surveillance stuff along the Rio Grande, or if someone that ran the equipment was helping people get across for a price. He said that he was going to talk to who ever was in charge the next morning, and thanked me for telling him. I felt pretty good about being able to help Dad. He seemed to be awfully frustrated about the way things were going at work, lately.

Both Jack and I were tired and turned in about nine. I think we were both asleep by the times our heads touched our pillows. Andy seemed tired, too. Of course, Andy always seemed tired, so I couldn't tell if he really worn out or if he was faking it. I went off to sleep dreaming about becoming a pilot. I made my decision then and there, if that girl, Kelli, could do it, then so could I.

————————

The next couple of days were pretty much the same as the first. By now, though, we had learned how to open and close—just like Luis. And our radio calls were improving fast. I also got to see all of the mistakes the student pilots made when they were shooting landings, as well being able to hear the commentary from the Instructors—I figured it might help when I got the chance to try it.

Cody got a little lock-box for the coke-money, which he decided to keep in a drawer in the mobile unit, so we didn't have to worry about someone stealing it from the other building. The mobile was also much stronger than that old shack. It was made out of metal and the glass part was super thick, making it almost impossible to break. A repair crew showed up on Tuesday to fix the damage the burglar caused. They replaced the broken glass, and put some kind of locks on the bottom of the windows which made them harder to open.

While the instructors were there, the three of us wandered around the area looking for interesting stuff. We did see a number of tarantulas on Wednesday afternoon, but since it wasn't mating season, they didn't do much—just lay around sunning. Jack spooked a big rattle snake the same day, and it made a heck of a noise. Boy did Jack back up in a hurry.

The rattler didn't try to attack him or anything, it just slithered away when we moved back from it. We did hear the herd of Javelina moving around over by the arroyo where we left Porky, but we didn't see hide nor hair of him. Just as well, Luis said, we don't want give the others a reason not to like him. I think he did miss the little guy, though, we could tell when we were out wandering around, and he really wanted to know if he was okay. There were also a million white-wing doves out there—boy could they fly. They stayed mainly around a big man-made pond that Luis called a tank. There was also a windmill there that pumped water into a big trough for cattle or horses, I guess. I never did see either one, neither had Luis. I was thinking that maybe, someone had built it just for the wildlife around there. Luis did tell us that deer wandered through there once in a while, but only in the fall. Whatever the reason, I decided; the windmill was a good idea.

The instructor, Bill Bates, was waiting for one last airplane—boring. It got delayed or something, because it was going to be an hour late. Then we heard Cody on the radio. "Hey, Bill, I heard you are stuck there for a while. Do suppose a couple of your helpers might want to shoot a couple of landings?"

Bill looked around at the three of us. We were all nodding like crazy. "Hi, Cody. I think you might talk one or two of them into it if you try real hard.

"Tell them to flip for firsts. I'm in my Swifty and will be there in a minute."

We immediately flipped. First odd man out, then who ever makes the call. Wouldn't you know it, Jack beat me again. "I won, I won," he screamed, as he jumped out the door and started acting like a nut.

"I can't believe it," I said to Luis. "He's the luckiest guy in the world."

Just then we saw the little silver Globe Swift turning final, about one half mile out. Cody squeaked it on the runway and was soon roaring back to pick up Jack. They were airborne before we knew it and started shooting landings about fifteen minutes later, after doing some practice maneuvers up north, according to Luis.

"That's a great airplane," Bill said, sounding real envious. "Some call it the poor man's P-51. They were built right after the second war, in 1946. A small company called Globe, a firm up in Ft. Worth, started making them at first, but, because the demand was so high, they had to get some help from a bigger outfit called, TEMCO. Between them, they must have made more than fifteen hundred of them in the first year or so. They quit making them in 1951, I think. Not too many of them around anymore.

It was a very modern airplane for its day: all metal, retractable gear, with a side-by-side cockpit configuration—using control sticks instead of wheels—just like a fighter. The Air Force almost bought it for a trainer, but couldn't sell the idea of a side-by-side cockpit to the generals. Of course, it was a tail-dragger too, so that didn't help. But mainly, they weren't sure it would work as well as the tried and true tandem trainers they'd always had. So the military bought the Beech

T-34 instead. It also had a tricycle gear, which was more forgiving to a novice pilot. The Swift ended up with a 160 horse power engine that would propel that little bird to over 200 mph. It's fully acrobatic and will stay up for almost four hours. It would have been a perfect military trainer. Cody's lucky to have one."

By that time, Cody was back in the traffic pattern. It was easy to tell which one had the controls—when Jack had the stick the airplane was bouncing around all over the place. After about five tries, though, he got it on the ground pretty good. He also made the last one. Luis told me to be next, that he might talk Cody into taking him home after we closed every thing up. I told him that I knew how to close up, and not to worry. It was pretty easy actually, and then Jack and I could talk to each other about flying on our way back to the base on the fire truck.

Pretty soon, Cody pulled up and dropped off Jack. I jumped in quickly and buckled my harness. Before you know it we were roaring down the runway. "Wow, Cody," I yelled over the engine noise, "This seems faster than the PT-22."

Cody nodded. "It is. Almost twice as fast." He leaned over and found the headset behind the seat. "Here, put this on, you can hear better." The intercom worked great, and I could hear Cody fine. He continued talking. "We're going to make a few maneuvers, first, and then do a stall series, so you'll know how the airplane feels when you lose lift. It's the most important thing you have to know when you are coming into land. He started with a couple of steep turns and did what he called a chandelle. It was a big old climbing steep turn that was really neat. Next, he did what he called a lazy eight. I don't know how to describe it exactly, but I think we made a figure eight and went up and down at the same time. Then he let me make some turns and dives and zooms. I wasn't too bad. I knew about the artificial horizon, so I checked it every once in a while to make sure I was straight and level.

Then, Cody took the controls and slowed the airplane down. He kept the power back until the airplane started to shake a little bit until it suddenly jerked and the nose went down abruptly. It felt like my stomach came up to my chin. "Eddie, that's what happens when the wings run out of lift. The airplane can't fly without enough air moving over the top of the wing—that's how a plane flies." He did it another time and I kept my hand lightly on the stick until I could feel the airplane quiver. "That's when you push forward on the stick and add power—when you feel the stick start to quiver." Then, he had me try it all by myself. I was doing okay, until it started to quiver. I added power, but didn't push forward fast enough. The nose started sideways, at first, and then dropped pretty wild. Cody took control quickly. You almost entered a spin. I'll give you a demo later. Then he let me try a stall again. I anticipated what was going to happen and caught it this time. "That one was perfect, Eddie. Let's go shoot a couple of landings."

He let me fly until we turned on final. He talked constantly, describing every part of the descent until we made our touchdown and took off again. "Okay, you got it, Eddie. Give me a landing. I bounced around the pattern he'd shown me and finally made it to the final approach. I couldn't seem to keep it lined up with the runway and we had to take it around when we got down to fifty feet. On the next approach Cody showed me how I could keep it straight, by keeping one wing down into the wind and using opposite rudder. When I turned final the next time, I kept it lined up. I was doing great until I got close to the ground. Then I started to over control the aircraft. "I've got it," Cody hollered and took it around. "Take it easy, Eddie. You don't have to hold onto the stick so tight. You fly best with the tips of your fingers, so you can feel every little movement. You can't do that when you are squeezing it tight." Boy, I was really sweating by now—flying is hard. He gave me the controls again and I made it all the way until we touched down. Cody kind of helped me keep it right during the landing roll and takeoff. Then we made our last approach. I did much better, this time, and managed to touchdown pretty smooth. Cody took over during the landing roll. "You will need to get some experience on the ground—a tail dragger is tough to taxi—easy to lose control. You're landings aren't too bad for the first time, and I think you have a good feel for a cross-wind." By that time we had made it back to the pad. Cody shut down the engine and we both got out. "Luis," he hollered, "As soon as Bill's ride gets here we can shut down this operation for the night. Why don't you let the boys do it while you supervise?" Luis nodded.

A few minutes later a Bonanza showed up to pick up Bill—the plane he was waiting for never made it. "Flying in style these days, huh, Bill?" Cody yelled. Bill hollered something back and waved. It must have been funny, because it broke Cody up. Probably one of those adult jokes that never seem to make much sense to me.

When the Bonanza left, Luis gave us a quick rundown on the shut down procedure. I had it down cold already, and told he and Cody to go ahead and takeoff—Jack nodded his agreement, conveying that he knew what to do. They smiled at our confidence and jumped in the Swift. I gave them my best professional sounding radio call. "Swift six two two, this is Tarantula, how do you read? Over."

Cody answered, "Roger, Tarantula, we read you five square."

"Swift six two two, you are cleared for takeoff runway three zero zero, winds two nine zero at six knots, altimeter two niner niner six, call leaving our control area."

"Tarantula, Swift six two two rolling, thanks for your help." With that he roared off down the runway and made a sharp climbing right turn. "Swift six two two departing control area, good-day." Then he added, "See you at home, Cowboys, ya done great today."

Jack checked out with Laredo, sounding really good, never making a mistake. Then we shut everything down. I got the flares and binoculars while Jack checked all of the switches off. Once everything was double checked, I locked the unit and we headed for the fire truck—talking a mile a minute about our adventures that day.

––––––––––––––––

On the way home the firemen sang like crazy. They were all Mexican Americans and knew lots of Mariachi songs. Pretty soon,

Jack and I joined in, adding our eeaaaahoo, yip, yip, yip, to the end of each chorus. It was a fun way to end the day, singing like they did. I was glad we had come to Laredo, and had the chance to learn about different cultural stuff.

The driver dropped us off where our bikes were parked. We jumped on them and headed for home. We talked the whole way back to the house, mostly about flying. One time, I reminded Jack that I told him we were going to have a fun time here, and that he was reluctant about coming. He admitted that it was having the best time he's ever had. I told him that I'd been worried for a while about bringing him here, but not anymore—that I really felt good about us sharing the fun with each other. He agreed, and said that I was still his best friend—forever.

———————

Both Mom and Dad were there when we got home. We told them about our day, kind of nonchalant, not wanting to make them think we were doing anything too special. Dad, in particular, was envious when we told him about flying in a Swift, but he was just as excited for us as Mom. They had already decided that we would go to the family restaurant, and Jack and I were elated—we really liked the food there.

Jack and I sat around the house that evening, just talking about flying. We had to mow the lawn in the morning, but neither of us minded—it was easy. We watched TV for a while, but it wasn't anywhere near as exciting as what we'd been doing. Finally, we gave up and went to bed. Andy trotted along behind us and jumped up on his pillow, ready for a little shut-eye.

I laid there in the dark, thinking. We were off until Friday. Cody had lined up another plane for us to wash, but other than that, we didn't have much going on.

Oh, yeah. We had to meet Victoria and her aunt on Sunday—ugh! Of course, Mom insisted that we meet them at the airport, and take she and her aunt out to dinner that night. I don't know why moms make their kids do that kind of stuff. Don't they know what a pain it is to clean up, wear your good clothes, and worry all through dinner if you were going to spill something on your shirt or pants? I'll bet she even makes Jack and I get haircuts on Saturday. Besides, we'll have to answer all the dumb question Mrs. Porter will ask about us being here and stuff. Oh, well. No sense fighting it. I'm plenty old enough to have learned that. No matter how much you try, you just can't get moms to give up on something they've made their mind up about. I guess it wouldn't be too bad having Victoria here. She can be fun sometimes. Anyway, I figure she will be pretty impressed that Jack and I are almost pilots. With that, I closed my eyes and went to sleep.

CHAPTER TWELVE

It was Monday morning right after breakfast. Jack and I were sitting on the back porch trying to calm down after a hectic weekend. Actually, it was more than a weekend; it was Friday, too—three days. Nothing had worked as planned, at least not for us.

First of all the Cessna, 150, Jack and I were going to wash Friday morning, turned out to be two Cessna, 150s. That wasn't so bad, we needed the extra money. Anyway, we had to stop in the middle of washing the first one, and start on the other, because the owner needed it by ten—something important came up.

By the time we got back to the one we had started on first, that owner came over and started telling us how he wanted it done. It took us at least an hour longer to finish because he kept stopping us to point out places he thought we'd missed. We didn't miss anything; actually, he just thought we did because he couldn't see very well in the hanger.

Man, you should have seen the coke bottle glasses he wore—I don't know how he could fly seeing as bad as he did.

Then, when we got home, Mom sent us to get haircuts. We rode our bikes down to the barber shop and it was jammed. It took us more than two hours to get finished. By the time we got home, we only had enough time to feed Andy and eat dinner. That wasn't so hot either. Mom fixed hot dogs because Dad wasn't going to be home on time.

Of course, Saturday got screwed up because Mom decided we needed new outfits to wear to meet Victoria. Man, I tell you, it was a hassle. The store was crowded and she had us trying on everything in the place. We finally got some gray dress-pants, and a couple of new shirts. They weren't too bad except we both knew we were going to spill something on them at dinner the next day, and Mom would grab a wet napkin to wash us off in front of everybody. Naturally that would embarrass us to death. At least dinner was good, Mom fixed fried chicken. I think she did it to make us feel better about meeting Victoria.

Sunday was really bad. First, we had to go to eight o'clock church so we could get to the airport by ten o'clock, when Victoria and her aunt got there. Of course, Mom got us up at dawn and made us shower and get dressed in our new outfits. She must have combed our hair fifty times during breakfast and at church. By the time we got to the airport my head was getting sore from all that combing.

At last the plane from Houston got there. It was a small Saab twin engine turbo prop. They parked pretty close to the gate and let the passengers off. I spotted Victoria and her aunt. They were dressed in pants, kind of casual—of course Mom wouldn't have believed me if I had said they weren't going to be dressed up. Oh, well. We all met and walked over to our car. Mrs. Porter looked like a dead-ringer for Victoria's mom. Then I got to thinking that she should, after all, they were sisters.

"How was your trip?" I asked Victoria after all of the meeting stuff was over.

Victoria smiled. "It was very nice, thank you. It only took about an hour. The plane was a little noisy, though."

What an opening. I went for it. "Boy, you think that's noisy, you should fly in a PT-22 sometime, like Jack and I did. We got to fly some, too."

She looked surprised. "A PT-22, what's that?"

"It's a World War II trainer with two open cockpits. You have to wear a leather helmet because your head is right out in the open. Cody let us fly, and he did loops, rolls, spins, and all kinds of neat stuff. Naturally, it was kind of scary, but we could handle it." Oops, I almost forgot, "And it's really, <u>really</u>, noisy." I looked at her closely to see if she was impressed.

She kind of nodded. "I guess all planes are a little noisy." Then she turned around quickly. "Who is Cody?"

"He's the best pilot in Texas. He owns the Lone Star Flying Service. That's the place Jack and I work. We'll take you over to meet him tomorrow if you want. He's really a neat guy. You will also meet Luis.

He works for Cody and is thirteen, not much older than us. We are all good friends, though, in spite of our age difference."

"Luis?" she questioned. "Is he a Mexican American?"

I nodded. "Yes. You'll like him."

Ah, oh. That gave her an opening. "By the way, how are you doing with your Spanish? I'll bet you can really understand a lot by now."

I looked down sheepishly, and was about ready to spill the beans when Jack came over.

"Hi Victoria, *Como esta usted, amiga?*"

Her eyes lit up. *"Es maravilloso. Juan hablo Espanol."* Then she started rattling off all kinds of stuff he didn't comprehend. Finally, she realized he didn't understand a word she was saying. "Oh, Jack, you don't really speak Spanish do you?" Then she looked at me. My eyes gave me away. "Oh, Eddie. You, too?"

"Just what you taught me in Florida," I confessed, then remembered a couple of words Luis taught me. "Well maybe a few other things, but not much. We've really been busy working and flying and everything. Way too busy for learning Spanish."

She shook her finger at me. "Eddie Matthews, I'm not going to give up on you. I know you can learn if you want to." Just then, Mom came over and we all got in the car. Of course, the three of us kids had to get in back, with Victoria in the middle. She started giving us Spanish lessons on the way to the BOQ apartment where they were staying. Man, I thought, this is going to be a long three weeks.

Mom still made us wear our good outfits to the restaurant that evening. Dad got off, for a change, and we went across the river to the Rincon de Viejo. Jack and I liked the place, but weren't looking forward to a barrage of Spanish lessons from Victoria all during dinner. We got there just before it got dark, and it didn't look quite so attractive as before. Oh, well, the food was good. Naturally, Victoria thought it was the neatest place in the world and started talking to anybody that would listen to her. At least that got her off our backs. Once it got dark and the lights were twinkling, it looked a lot better. Victoria got cabrito, like the rest of us, and proceeded to give us a lesson on the history of goats—at least that was in English. When the Mariachi came we helped them with the eeaaaahoo, yip, yip, yip, which Victoria had never done before. At least we had something over her. The cabrito and stuff was super, so everything wasn't bad—but by the time we dropped them off at the base, we were a little sick of Spanish lessons.

So that's how it was for the last three days. Oh, I almost forgot. Andy tried to dig Oscar, the Armadillo out of his hole, and got super dirty. I had to give him a bath, and was told to figure out how they could co-exist. Now how would I know that, I wondered? I couldn't make a fence or Oscar couldn't get in there either. Maybe I would think of something later. Well, one day down, twenty to go. Boy, this is going to be a long visit.

Things had pretty much settled down by Tuesday. Victoria and her aunt had to take Monday off so they could get settled. I couldn't understand why they needed a whole day to unpack two suitcases, but I didn't worry about it. I had just about given up trying to understand females. Jack and I were scheduled to get a tour of the language school and then have lunch with Victoria. Afterwards, we were going to take her over to the flight line to meet Cody, and then show her Cody's Lair and his toys.

Jack and I got to the base early, and talked Luis into joining us for the tour of the language school. He took us up on it, and said he wanted us to meet his mother. I think he wanted to meet Victoria, too.

We were a little early, so Luis took us to the administrative office to meet his mom. She was really nice, her name was Alicia. I could tell she was real proud of Luis just by the way she looked at him. She pointed to a picture of his dad on her desk. "Wow, Luis," I exclaimed. "You two are like peas in a pod. You look just like a younger version of him."

"His name was Carlos," his mom said, smiling, agreeing with me. "They are a lot alike, more than just looks." She abruptly put the picture down and took a breath to steady her emotions. Then she escorted us down to where Victoria and Mrs. Porter were located.

Mrs. Porter greeted all of us, and introduced Luis to Victoria. He shook hands with her and gave me kind of a funny, knowing look afterwards. Then we started our tour of the language school.

The school was the entire lower level of what used to be a long two story building for housing bachelor student officers. There was a large briefing room on one end that would accommodate at least fifty people. Then there were six smaller classrooms designed for three students plus one instructor. At the other end was a large language laboratory full of cubicles, where students put on earphones and listened to their lessons in Spanish.

Upstairs, there were sixteen individual rooms connected by a bathroom. Each student had his own room and shared the bath. There was also a place to do laundry, and a recreation room with couches and chairs for watching TV, as well as a pool table.

It was pretty nice. Heck, the students had someone to clean up after them, make their bed, and only had to walk across the street to the cafeteria. Their classes lasted six weeks, and concentrated on specific things they would be asking people that wanted to cross the border. No one spoke English when they entered the school area—everything was in Spanish. Boy, no wonder Victoria knew how to speak, her aunt spoke Spanish half the time.

We got to see everything and listened in on a couple of classes. After the tour, the four of us kids went outside to take a break. Just when we got comfortable, relaxing on the steps, we were almost run over by nine students on their way to a big old van that had parked out front. The students were carrying briefcases and a couple of other big old black suitcase like things. The van was painted green and gray, and had United States Border Patrol in big letters on the sides. The driver had on some kind of official looking uniform and opened the door for them when they arrived. Pretty soon, they roared off.

"What was that all about, Victoria?" Jack asked.

"Oh. The students go down to the main interrogation center across the bridge and practice talking with people coming across the border. They go twice a week after the first week they're here."

Jack was scratching his head. "What for? What's all that junk they're carrying?"

Victoria continued, "They talk mostly with documented workers, and have an expert there in case they make a mistake. It's the best practice in the world talking to native speakers. It's much easier than talking student to student. Native speakers talk much faster, don't always use the correct words, and have different dialects. It's much different. For example, a Mexican from the Yucatan has a distinctly different dialect than that of someone from Monterrey or Laredo, who sometimes throw in a little English when they talk. My aunt thought it up, and it works great. Oh, and the junk they're carrying is tape recorders, and projectors—extra stuff to help them."

Jack persisted. "Why would they need that stuff if all they are going to do is talk?"

"Oh, never mind, Jack. I'll show you later how some of the stuff is used if you are <u>really</u> interested." Jack backed off with that. Then Luis stepped in.

"Wow. I never paid much attention to the way people speak Spanish. I can tell the difference, now that I think about it, but I never thought about it that way." Then surprise came over his face. "Hey, maybe that's why I have such a hard time understanding people from Canada, or the Northeastern part of the United States. They do talk different, and I've had trouble understanding what they wanted sometimes. I guess it works both ways."

"Exactly," Victoria said, knowingly. "I still have trouble understanding Catalonian Spanish, and some of the dialects from South America. It just takes practice and a trained ear."

"How do you practice?" Luis asked. "How in the world do you train your ear?"

"Well," Victoria said, "Last year when I came to visit Aunt Virginia, I got really bored because I didn't know anybody my age to be with, so I just spent most of my extra time in the Language Lab."

Luis looked surprised. "Do you mean you have tapes with all of the different dialects on them?"

"Well, not all of them. But we have quite a few. And not just in Spanish. We have all kinds of tapes. Practically every language in the world."

Jack butt in. "Hey, it's eleven-thirty, the cafeteria line's open. Let's go eat lunch." He jumped up and started down the stairs. "Well, are you coming?" We all laughed and followed him to the cafeteria.

Luis kind of pulled me back when we got to the door, letting Jack and Victoria go ahead. "Hey, Eddie. I can see why you said Victoria was okay. I think she's pretty neat, too. I can tell she likes you. Did you know that?"

I was kind of shocked. "What do you mean?"

He acted kind of perturbed. "She likes you," he said, raising his voice a little, then lowered it—kind of whispering. "You know, girl likes boy? She looks at you all the time and just grins—that means she likes you."

"It does? I never heard that before."

"Well it does, my Mom told me."

Hmm. Now that was really a surprise. I felt kind of good about it, though, but wasn't sure if I could believe Luis. I mean, how could he know for sure? He hardly knows her. Oh, nuts. Now I'll have to ask Mom. Of course, she'll grin, and say all that same old just-be-nice stuff and wink a lot. But I need to find out if I'm suppose to say anything back, like, I like you too, or smile at her, or something like that. After all, I wasn't very experienced around girls. Man, sometimes growing up is a hassle.

————————————

After lunch we walked over to the flight line and visited Cody's Lair. Victoria's eyes lit up when we walked in and saw his toys. "Aren't they beautiful?" she said, as she sauntered toward them. She stopped and touched the propeller on the Swift while she gazed at the airplane. She turned to Jack and I. "You both have flown this airplane?" We nodded, proudly. Then she walked back to the Ryan PT-22. "Oh, isn't this one cute," she said, walking over to the aft cockpit. "Is this the one that's supposed to be so noisy?"

"It's noisy all-right, but not what I'd call cute," I added, going over to tell her about the stuff in the cockpit.

"Well, I think it's cute. What fun you must have had doing all of those acrobatic maneuvers."

I nodded like mad. Then Jack butt in and started telling her all about acrobatics. Luis just stood in the background with a big smile on his face, watching us make fools of ourselves.

In the meanwhile, the bright yellow Beechcraft Staggerwing caught her eye. She hurried over and touched the left wing, then followed it to the cabin. She looked inside. "Wow! This one is my favorite. Have you flown in this one? Quick, tell me about it."

Jack and I looked dejected. "No, we haven't been up in her, yet." But Luis has, haven't you Luis?" Jack said.

Luis ambled over. "Yes. I've been up in it a few times. This one is Cody's favorite, too," he said, looking at Victoria.

"Tell me about it. Please, Luis," she pleaded.

"Well, I usually let Cody tell you about one of his toys, but I guess it wouldn't hurt to tell you a little bit. Here, sit down, and I'll fill you in."

We all selected a folding chair from the stack leaning against the back of the hanger, and then sat down in kind of a circle, facing Luis. "This aircraft was designed by a guy named, Ted Wells, way back in 1932. He was encouraged by a man named, Walter Beech. Anyway, Beech, who founded Beechcraft Aviation, thought there would be a market for a fast luxurious light transport. Wells came up with this designed, called the D-17. It was a five place biplane with a backward staggered wing—now you understand the name; all other biplanes have the top wing forward. It also had a retractable landing gear, another first for a biplane. Because it was so sleek, the airplane would cruise between 170-200 mph, had a seven hundred mile range, and could reach 18,000 feet. The wings are a little over thirty feet long and the whole airplane is only twenty-six feet long. It's light, too, only a hair over two thousand pounds, and was faster than most fighters when first introduced. The cabin is all upholstered in leather, and is also insulated so it wouldn't be so noisy—that's the luxury part. It was equipped with very modern instrumentation for it's day, too."

Luis paused for a minute to catch his breath. "Cody's aircraft is a later model, made in 1939 for the Army Air Corps. This one was based in Paris, and flew dignitaries from our embassy to London, Rome, and other important places right after the city was liberated in 1944. This aircraft has a bigger engine, a 450 horse power Pratt-Whitney, R-985, allowing this baby to cruise at 202 mph. It has a range of 785 miles and will fly at 20,000 feet. One of the pilots who flew it, an air attaché, bought it right after the war and had it crated up and shipped home. Unfortunately, he was killed when his transport aircraft crashed in Greenland on his way back to the States. Cody said the aircraft just sat in the attaché's folk's barn for close to fifteen years. Then some buddy of Cody's told him about it and he talked the parents into selling it to him. The restoration work began a few years later, after Cody could afford it. This aircraft took almost three years to get in the shape it's in today—totally rebuilt—and perfect.

"That's about it. It is really neat to fly in. Cody doesn't share much of the flying time, thought, since it's his favorite. I'm sure he will take you up. He usually flies it to San Antonio every couple of months when he visits Alamo Air, the outfit that flies Lear-jets down here to Tarantula. That's where he flies it the most."

We all had a thousand questions, and it must have taken Luis an hour to answer them. Afterward, we wandered back over to the cafeteria for a drink. Wouldn't you know it, Victoria ordered orange juice instead of coke—no wonder Mom liked her. We sat around for a while, and planned for our visit to Tarantula Field the next day. We wanted to show Victoria how neat it was.

Jack and I hopped on our bikes and arrived home just in time to feed Andy. He hadn't attacked Oscar that day, so I guess I was off the hook for a while with Mom. After settling down, we sat on the back porch for before dinner to think about our day. That's when Dad came home. He immediately started complaining to Mom about work.

Mom saw him fuming and opened the conversation. "What's wrong at work now?"

That's all Dad needed. He started pacing up and down and griped and griped and griped. "I've never been so frustrated in my life, Janet. The FBI got word about someone else supposedly coming through Laredo. I'm beginning to think they must be wrong. We've been over every piece of equipment we own, and have re-looked at our tapes until they are almost worn out. There is just nothing on them that would prove anything—zero!

Mom questioned, "What about the burglar at Tarantula. Did the ground surveillance people find anything there?"

Dad slugged his hand with his fist. "No! Of course, not! A total dead end. They're not even going to follow up on the thing because they think it would have been impossible for anyone to sneak across the river around here—that it must have been some down-on-their-luck burglar from around here. Everything and everybody connected with this thing seems to be perfect. The ground guys said they have checked out every piece of equipment they've got, and have reviewed their surveillance cameras film I don't know how many Times—five or six at least. The people check out, too. Everybody is as loyal as they can be. This thing is driving an awful lot of people nuts: The Agency's mad, the Attorney General's mad, the Homeland Defense leader is mad, the President's mad—everybody's mad. And I'm mad, too." He reached in the fridge for a beer.

"Calm down, Jim. It won't do any good to rant and rave about it—but I can't help but feel there is an answer there somewhere, it's got to be."

He grabbed, Mom. "Oh, honey. I know I'm acting crazy, but this thing is soooo frustrating. Do you know what I mean?" She grabbed him and gave him a hug.

There they go again, I thought. I wonder what they think hugs are going to do. Maybe I ought to get our gang to thinking about this thing. I still believe that guy who stole the money out there at Tarantula is more important than all of those experts think. Maybe we can help Dad—who knows? Cody might help, too.

We had a great dinner. Sirloin steak and baked potatoes. Mmmm. Mom even made artichokes which are fun, tearing off the leafs and dipping them in lemon-butter. Jack had never had one, so he learned something else today. We also had fresh strawberries and some neat-tasting sauce. Boy, it was good.

After dinner, Victoria's aunt called and talked with Mom for a while. I guess she was okay with Victoria going with us to Tarantula tomorrow, only she wanted to make sure we all wore boots, long sleeved shirts, and big old Mexican straw hats—to keep the sun off. She said she had extra hats for us, that Victoria would bring them in the morning. And she was also sending an ample supply of sun-screen. Mom filled us in about what we were going to have to wear, even digging long sleeved blue shirts out of some box she had stashed in the closet. Jack and I looked at each other after she finished. Man, I tell you, when grown-up women get together about watching out for kids, they go nuts. Heck, we hadn't gotten sunburned or anything so far, had we? Oh, well. No sense fighting it—we'd lose.

With that, we hit the sack. Andy followed us into the bedroom and got his bed ready while we were washing up and brushing our teeth. It was going to be a long day tomorrow, so we decided not to do too much talking before going to sleep. After about thirty minutes of grumbling we decided to get a little shut-eye.

CHAPTER THIRTEEN

I knew the morning wasn't going to be great, and I was right. Wearing those stupid shirts and hats was going to be bad enough. But then, on top of that, Mrs. Porter called and said she wanted to drive us out there, that she wouldn't mind seeing the place. After hearing her say it, Mom decided that she wanted to see the place too, of course. I complained to Jack, "Man, what else can happen?"

Before Jack could answer, Mom joined us. "Oh, quit complaining. You sound just like you did when you went to see the planets. That worked out okay, didn't it?"

I had to admit, she was right there. "Yeah, I guess so," I said, not wanting to sound too agreeable. "But we can't be late; we've got to open up before the instructors get there."

She looked around, "When's that?"

"I'm not real sure. About nine-thirty or ten, something like that. Luis will know, maybe we should ask him."

"I don't think that will be necessary. Luis already knows Mrs. Porter's driving. He's going with us."

Now she tells me. It's almost like she sets me up, I complained to myself. "Well, I hope Mrs. Porter knows the road is kind of rough," I said, hoping Mom hadn't thought about that.

"Oh, she knows. That's why she's taking us in the school van. It's heavy-duty, I think, or something like that. Anyway, it will not be a problem because of the vehicle."

I sighed to myself, thinking I was never going to beat Mom ever—at least when it came to this kind of stuff. It's like kids our age are born to lose when they deal with their moms.

Then, after about giving up on her, Mom made really great sandwiches for everybody, and started making bacon and eggs, one of my all-time favorite breakfasts. "Oh, boy, bacon and eggs. Mmmm." Jack was licking his chops by the time Mom served him. Sometimes, Jack reminded me of the way Andy looked when I was getting ready to feed him. "Great breakfast, Mom," I said, after washing my plate and placing it on the counter. She gave me her super smile, which always got to me, making me feel bad for doubting her motives.

Jack followed suit. "Great breakfast, Mrs. Matthews. I've never had better," he added, never missing a chance to suck up.

After breakfast, Mom checked us out, smeared some sunscreen on our faces, and we headed for the base. She started to park in front of the Language School, and got cut off by an old pickup truck. Mom slammed on the brakes. "Did you see that?"

"It's just Pedro, Mom. He delivers coke, pop, and water to offices around the base. He brings stuff over to Cody's office, and even comes out to Tarantula once in a while. He's old, that's all."

She mumbled, while backing up and parking behind him. "Well, he needs to be more careful—even if he is old. That spot isn't even marked as a loading zone. I have just as much right to park there as he does." She continued griping.

Just then, Mrs. Porter drove up in a big old white van. We all piled out and waited for her to pull in behind us. It had seats for ten people, and did look pretty heavy-duty. They had already been down to the hanger to get Luis, so we all got in and took off for Tarantula.

Victoria started passing out hats right after we hit the highway. They were huge! The brims must have been two feet wide, and they drooped down almost past your shoulders. Guess we didn't have to worry about the sun when we were wearing these hats, I thought, all we had to worry about was seeing—anything.

"These are field-workers hats," Luis said, trying his on. "They really do shield you from the sun, and make your head cooler, too. Thanks, Mrs. Porter, these are great." Oh, man, another thing to worry about. We'll never get to take them off, I thought, as I hunkered down in my seat—trying my best to be patient until the trip was over.

Jack punched me on the shoulder, and leaned over, whispering. "Eddie, did you see what happened back there with Pedro's truck and that Border Patrol van?"

"No, what happened?"

"I saw the drivers change coats and hats."

"You, what? Be serious, Jack. You were seeing things. Why would Pedro want to do that? You're nuts." Jack shrugged, and was about to say something else just as we got there. I told Mrs. Porter to park next to the pad by the mobile unit.

We got out, and Luis gave Mom and Mrs. Porter a tour of the place before opening up the unit—mainly pointing things out. The women looked a little skeptical, but seemed to accept the sparse surrounding.

Luis got out his keys and invited the two of them over to the mobile control. He opened it up and showed them the way we set up things, and got everything ready. They were really impressed. I mean, <u>really</u> impressed with his professionalism. He did everything but shoot a flare. He couldn't do that until the fire truck showed up. When they got out, I climbed in the unit to listen for the instructors to call. I didn't have to wait long. "Tarantula tower, this is Cessna five two seven, how do you read?"

I picked up the mike and answered. "I read you five square, five two seven. Cleared to runway zero three zero, winds zero one zero at two knots, altimeter two niner niner eight." Just then the fire truck arrived and roared down the runway. I continued with my call. "Five two seven, the runway is being checked now, call one mile final for clearance to land. The fire truck finished their sweep and was pulling into their parking place when the instructors called back.

"Tarantula, five two seven, one mile."

"Roger, five two seven, cleared to land, taxi-back approved."

"Roger." I put down the mike and took a look at them through the binoculars. Then, I realized that Victoria was in there with me. I handed her the binoculars, "Want to take a look?"

She watched the plane until it got pretty close, then she saw the pilot squeak it on the runway right in front of us.

Her eyes lit up. She handed the binoculars back to me. "Wow, Eddie," she said, "You are really good at this." She watched in awe while the Cessna made it's turn around and parked right next to us. She looked back at me. "Oh, Eddie, flying is neat." I thought she was going to give me a hug or something, until everyone congregated next to the unit to meet each other.

"I guess we better go join everybody," I said. She gave me kind of a strange look and nodded. Then we joined the others. Mom and Mrs. Porter hung around until the first student started practicing landings. Then they decided that we weren't going to up and die or something and left. At last we were on our own.

Victoria could see right away that shooting landings wasn't too exciting, so we gave her a real tour of the place—of course, she made us wear those stupid hats and rub on more sun stuff.

First, we showed her where we let Porky loose, and then wandered around looking for spiders and snakes. Finally, we found two big old tarantulas together. "I think they're going to mate," Luis said. We watched while they kind of talked to each other with their feelers. Then, finally, the little one jumped on the top of the other. They just stayed there—doing nothing.

"That's it?" Jack asked. Luis nodded. "But I thought you said something happened?"

Luis sat back, leaning against a mesquite tree. "Just keep on watching."

Pretty soon, the little one got off, and just sat there for a minute. Then, suddenly, the big one jumped on him and gave him a big bite. "She just killed him," Luis said, "pretty soon she will eat him up."

Victoria leaned forward. "Wow, I knew the Praying Mantis did that, but I didn't realize the Tarantula did too." Luis nodded that they did.

I was wondering what they were talking about until the female spider started to gobble him up. "Man, that's pretty dirty," I said, not wanting to understanding what was happening.

Victoria gave me that knowing look. "It's just nature," she said, "The mother's just programmed to look out for her babies, they will need nourishment to make the eggs strong, and so the babies can survive when they hatch."

Jack butt in. "Who programmed her, some cannibal-voodoo-witch-doctor or something?" Victoria didn't answer; she just gave him her look.

"Heck, this is no fun," Jack said, "Let's go eat our lunch.

"Good idea," I replied. I wasn't too enthralled with what had just happened either, and besides, I wanted to talk to everybody about helping Dad.

We went back to the main building and got our sandwiches out of the fridge. We pulled up some old folding chairs and started eating. After we were settled, I told them the story about the terrorist the FBI had caught in Dallas, and that he confessed he'd entered the country through Laredo. I told them that Jack and I overheard Dad talking about it—that was how we knew.

"This stuff is probably real secret, I think. We can't tell anybody about it." Then I explained that nobody seemed to be able to tell how the bad guy was able to get across the border. Then, when the FBI, and the CI...Government Agency Dad works for, heard about another terrorist being there, they were more concerned than ever. "I guess these are really bad people," I added, just to make sure they knew this was important. "Dad said that the FBI found a suitcase full of money and another filled with all kinds of plans, secret directions, and stuff like that at the captured man's apartment. They think there are more of them, and the group might be planning to do something bad at the DFW Airport, or poison the public water supply."

Everybody was wide-eyed with my story. Then I added, "I think that the guy that broke in here might somehow be connected with the terrorists, Luis. Of course, the experts on border surveillance don't even think it is worth looking into, according to Dad. So, I thought we might keep our eyes open and maybe we can help them out." Everyone was quiet for a moment—even Jack.

Luis spoke up, having a questioning look on his face. "Why would a terrorist steal coke money from an old rickety building like this— especially if he already had a suitcase full of it?"

Everyone looked at me for an answer. I threw up my hands, "Heck, I don't know. Maybe he couldn't open the case without it blowing up or something—maybe he didn't have the password—or a key—who knows?" I shrugged my shoulders, then thought of something. "Do you think someone could pick him up from here—fly him up to Dallas or somewhere like that? Maybe he was just waiting for a ride."

Jack answered. "But how would he get here? I mean across the border. Didn't your dad say that the experts hadn't seen anybody?"

Luis held up his hand. "Hold it. Someone watches every plane that comes in here—either the instructors or us. I don't think anybody could stop and pick up a passenger without one of us seeing it, don't you? Besides, if they stopped in the middle of the night or some other odd-ball hour when we're not here, your Dad's planes would see an airplane landing wouldn't he?" I nodded my agreement.

Nuts, there went another theory, I thought. "Wait a minute," Luis said. "Sometimes a Learjet stops at the other end of the field and parks on the pad down there. They shut down the aircraft and have the new student go through all of the start procedures and stuff. I guess it would be possible to pick someone up, but the whole crew would have to be in on it."

Hmmm, I thought. "If it is possible, then maybe we should look around here again. Maybe we missed something when we thought he was just some wet-back that had sneaked across the border."

"Good idea," Luis said, jumping up, leading the way. We all tossed our napkins and stuff in the trash and went over by the window where the burglar had broken in. "Let's see, he came in here and went to the refrigerator, then he must have left. If he had wanted to sleep in the storage room in this building, then why didn't he just use this door?" He pointed at the door in the corner. "There weren't any dirty tracks, so he must have left—most likely because he was hungry. He could have walked down the road a couple of miles to a gas station on highway, 59, bought some food with the money he stole, and returned." Jack and I agreed. Victoria just listened, wide-eyed.

Luis led us into the other building, and opened it up. "Okay, he must have come back here later, after he ate, and broken this window, found a blanket, and went to sleep in the back room—where it would be warmer. Nothing ever goes on over here, so he knew he'd be pretty safe. The next morning, he woke up and went back out into the wilderness area north of the field to wait for his ride."

Jack spoke up. "Boy, Luis. You ought to be a detective. What you said really sounds like it would work."

Finally, Victoria entered the conversation. "I'm not sure about all of the details, Luis, but it sounds like you have made a good case. What I can't figure out is how the terrorist got here in the first place. Especially since he must have been carrying two suitcases full of stuff. He would have to get here someway, wouldn't he? He must have been given a ride by somebody. He needed help, right?"

Those were good questions, I thought. I knew Victoria was quick about some things, but I didn't know she was that quick. I interrupted. "Wait a minute; I tossed an old letter or something into the trash in the other room. Maybe we ought to take a better look at it—if it's still there."

I ran to the trash can and dug around for a second or two until I found the paper. I took a look at it and saw nothing but squiggly writing or something like it. "Let me see it," Victoria said, suddenly looking serious. I handed it to her. She looked up abruptly, "This is Arabic writing, or Dari, or something close to it." We all just stood there, thinking about what she said. I don't think any of us really thought there was an <u>actual</u> terrorist here. But this was kind of scary—this wasn't a game. We all looked around at each other. Our eyes must have been as big as saucers. **WOW!**

After we calmed down we tried to decide what to do. "We can't tell my parents," I implored. "They would kill me. Jack too," I added for effect, making sure Jack was on my side. "We could really look stupid if we get everybody excited and then find out we're wrong. We need to check things out first—then maybe we could tell them."

Luis spoke up. "What do you mean, check things out?"

"Well, I think we should wait until they run a Learjet in here. Then one of us can hide up at the north end and see what they do. Then we would know."

Everybody nodded their approval. "But what's that going to prove, even if someone did get on the jet," Jack said, "He still could just be a wet-back. We still need to find out how someone could get across the river." Suddenly, his eyes lit up. "Wait a minute. Eddie, remember this morning I told you I saw Pedro change coats and hats with the Border Patrol driver? Maybe that has something to do with it."

I was just about to tell Jack to shut up when Luis piped in. "Pedro, you saw Pedro this morning? You couldn't have, he isn't even in Laredo anymore, and he sold his business about a month ago and moved back to Mexico. What's going on? Do you even know what Pedro looks like?"

Jack shrugged. "All I know is the guy driving the pickup with Pedro painted on the side changed jackets and hats with the driver from the Border Patrol van."

Everyone was silent for a minute, and then Victoria spoke. "Would it be possible to smuggle a terrorist across the river on the Border Patrol van?" Then her eyes lit up. "Maybe it's the driver. I'll bet nobody every checks the driver's papers. He could simply drive across the river when he brings the students back and bring his suitcases with him. I'll bet none of the experts would even think about something so simple. I think Jack's right. The drivers exchange positions when they get to the base, then the terrorist gets someone to drop him off when the pickup delivers coke and stuff out here. Obviously there are more people involved. The question is who?"

Well, we didn't have time to ponder the situation; it was almost time for us to close. We gathered in a circle and held hands. Then we agreed that we wouldn't talk to anyone about it except maybe Cody—and that was only until we had some proof and needed some advice. Then we made assignments. Victoria was going to check out the language on the letter we found, and then snoop around the school, to see if she could get an idea about the drivers of the Border Patrol van. Luis was going to check into the Pedro operation, and find out who owned them now, how many drivers they had, and find out if they had a schedule that always coincided with the Border Patrol van. Jack and I were going to casually talk with Dad to see if he would tell us more about what was happening from the government side of the house. Then, we were all going to come to Tarantula when the next Learjet was scheduled to be there, and get the proof.

We went about our closing-up jobs, and soon watched the last instructor depart for home on a Cessna 172. Then we quickly shut off the power and locked everything. Since Victoria had never ridden on a fire truck, we had talked Mom and Mrs. Porter out of coming back to pick us up. Victoria really thought it was neat, of course, and was even singing along with the firemen and us by the time we got home.

By the time Jack and I walked in the door we were whipped. We did our chores, ate dinner, and went to our room to think—keeping an ear out for Dad, in case he started griping again. Andy gave up early, and took a little before bed time nap. Both of us didn't say much, we just did some heavy duty thinking about this terrorist thing.

———————————

I got up early the next morning and joined Mom and Dad for breakfast. Jack decided to stay in bed for a while longer, so I could talk with my folks alone. I told them I had overheard them talking about some terrorist sneaking across the border the other day, and wondered what it was all about. Dad basically told me the story, but left out things like what organization the terrorist worked for, the documents and the money, and what kinds of things they might be targeting. I didn't push him, as Mom wasn't real happy with the way the conversation was going. I could tell she didn't want me to worry about some terrorist running around by the way she always bit her lip when she was worried. I changed the subject by mentioning to Dad that our whole gang had been at Tarantula the day before, and all had fun. He asked a couple of questions about Victoria, mainly about how I treated her—saying that he always wanted me to be a gentleman around girls.

Then I cautiously injected. "Hey, Dad. Did Mom tell you about that old guy Pedro almost running into us yesterday with his pickup? You know about Pedro, don't you?"

Dad's eyes lit up. "Janet, what happened?"

"Oh, it was nothing. I was just about to pull in at the language school and a pickup truck cut right in front of me. I guess I was kind of surprised." There was a pause. "Mad, too," she laughed. "He made me mad," she pouted, "He took my parking place."

Dad burst out laughing. "Ha, you lost your temper, didn't you? Pedro probably didn't even see you. I think he must be at least eighty." He shook his head. "He does have a reputation for being a bad driver from the people who work on the base. I guess you wouldn't have known to look out for him."

Mom was starting to laugh, too. "Well, the least you could have done was warned me." She pretended to be mad.

Dad picked up his plate, and headed for the sink. "Come to think of it, I don't think that will be a problem much longer. I heard that he was going to sell the business."

I quickly butted in. "Dad, does Pedro deliver stuff to your area, too. It seems like he goes all over the base."

Dad nodded. "Yes. He's an institution around here. He's one of the few people that is allowed in our area without a special security badge, although he is escorted by someone anytime he enters one of the buildings."

"I guess Cody would know if he sold his business," I said, getting up from the table. "Sorry, Mom, I didn't want to get you in trouble. Want me to wash my dishes?"

She gave me a big grin. "No, you don't have to wash them. And I'm not in any trouble. It's your dad who's in trouble." She gave him one of her looks. He winked back. Oh, man. There they go again.

I hurried back to the bedroom and woke up Jack. I told him that Dad said Pedro could go into his area without any special badge. "That means someone else could probably go in there too. Heck, you can't see who's driving because the windows have all of that dark sun shade stuff on them. Then they would know when the aircraft were on the ground and when they were flying."

201

Jack yawned. "Is that important?"

I shrugged. "Heck, I don't know. It might be. I guess the driver could call and tell a pilot somewhere else when the surveillance aircraft were on the ground, and he could fly across the border undetected."

Jack ate breakfast and then we just messed around the house for a while. We had two airplanes to wash right after lunch, so the gang was going to meet at the hanger and discuss what we had found out.

Andy had been harassing Oscar again, so I came up with a little tunnel arrangement made out of big tile pipe, that would allow him to get to his burrow without being attacked by my inquisitive schnauzer. Jack and I ate lunch about eleven-thirty and took off for the base on our bikes, eager to talk with everybody.

We all met at the cafeteria and got a coke—even Victoria and Luis. I told Luis about what Dad had said about the access Pedro had to his part of the base. Then Luis told us that Cody said Pedro had sold his business just three weeks ago to some guy from San Antonio. The new owner hasn't been around himself, and has been using a lot of different drivers until he finds someone to run the operation. Finally, Victoria informed us that the letter I pulled out of the trash was written in Arabic—that it was basically an index for a booklet. She said the index mentioned everything from how to get fake identification to the clothes they should wear to fool Americans.

"Wow," Luis said. "Did it say anything about blowing up stuff or poisoning water?"

Victoria shook her head. "No, but it was only the first page, there were probably a lot more pages."

I jumped in. "Victoria, did you happen to see the driver of the Border Patrol van?"

"No," she answered, "They weren't scheduled to come this morning. But I did follow the driver of Pedro's truck into the building, and watched him while he dropped off water and coke at the refrigerator in the recreation room. One of the janitors said hello, and he answered. He certainly wasn't Mexican—he spoke some sort of South American dialect."

All of us were pretty tense. "Luis, did you find out from Cody when the next Learjet is going to be at Tarantula?"

"Yes. Cody said there were two of them scheduled day after tomorrow, about noon."

With that, we went over to the flight line to wash the airplanes Cody had lined up. Victoria came with us, saying that she wanted to give it a try. We had a Cessna 150, and an old Ercoupe, a vintage two place aircraft from the forties. Luis cranked up the sprayer and we got going. Victoria helped with every task, fitting in well. She was a really good worker, and became part of our team—well, not really a member of the Cody's Lair team, she'd have to wait until she flew with Cody to earn that honor.

We finished in about two hours or so, and dropped by Cody's office to introduce Victoria to him. They really seemed to hit it off, and talked up a storm. When we were leaving, he loaned us his four walkie-talkie radios so we could always keep in contact with each other and practice radio calls, explaining that the radios had a range of almost thirty miles when they were charged up, and we could call his office, too, and even leave a message for him. That meant that we could call each other just like using cell-phones—neat. Luis had told Cody a little bit about our terrorist theory, and he promised to keep quiet as long as we weren't in trouble.

I asked Cody what he thought about Victoria when I was leaving. He said, "Eddie, if you threw that little girl in a pond, you could skim sweet off of the top for a week." I wasn't too sure what he meant by that, but I guessed he thought she was pretty nice. It probably had something to do with that old saying about girls being: sugar and spice and everything nice. What was it about boys? Oh, yeah: snakes and snails and puppy dog's tails. Whatever, I guessed Cody liked her. Actually, come to think of it, she could be pretty sweet.

We were about ready to go, when Cody stopped us. "You guys want to go to San Antonio with me tomorrow?"

We all looked at each other, and then Luis asked, "In the Staggerwing?"

Cody grinned. "Sure. I thought it was time y'all got a ride in her."

"Yes!" we all screamed in unison. "What time?"

"Eight o'clock at my office, Cowboys. Don't be late," he said, walking out. We just stood there in disbelief.

Victoria was awe-struck. "Does this mean I am going to get to fly?"

"Yes," I said. "In the Staggerwing. You're favorite airplane. It's going to be great."

We all danced around like fools. Finally, we calmed down. Luis said he would walk Victoria back to the school, so Jack and I grabbed our bikes and started peddling for home. We all headed off with the same dream in our head—thinking about flying in the neatest airplane in the world.

When we got home, both of ran in the kitchen to tell Mom. Jack wanted to telephone home, but Mom convinced him that he should wait until after he flies. That took off some of the excitement for him, but he got over it when Mom showed us what we were having for dinner—Roast turkey. "What's the occasion, Mom?"

"There isn't an occasion. It's just what they had on sale at the supermarket today. I thought we all deserved something special."

"Are you making dressing, too, Mrs. Matthews?" Jack said, almost salivating.

"Yes, boys. I'm fixing all of the trimmings—including pumpkin pie."

"Oh, Boy," we hollered as we ran out to the backyard. We kind of played around with each other, wrestling and horsing around, until Andy joined us and started biting at our legs. I grabbed him and played with him for a minute. He finally broke away and started tearing around the whole backyard as fast as he could run. After that, we were all tired, and just sat down in the shade to wait for dinner.

Then a good idea hit me. I decided to shower right then, so I didn't have to get up so early in the morning. Jack decided to clean up, too. Afterwards, we put on shorts and tee-shirts, and joined Mom in the kitchen. Golly, it really smelled good in there. "Need any help, Mom?"

"Oh, thank you, Eddie. How about setting the table. Might as well use the good stuff," she added. "We might as well make it an occasion." With that, she grabbed a bottle of wine from the rack and put it in the fridge.

Jack decided to give me a hand, so we busied ourselves fixing the table. We had just about finished when Dad got home. He went through the whole thing with Mom about why we were having the turkey, so I don't need to tell that part over again. About thirty minutes later, Mom sat the turkey on the table. Boy, did it look good. She also had green beans, sweet potatoes, and dressing—and cranberry sauce, too.

Jack spoke up. "Boy am I happy I didn't eat too much for lunch today." I agreed with him, and watched while he sniffed the air just like Andy. I was waiting for him to lick his chops when Mom called.

Dad carved the turkey after we said Grace. Jack and I got huge helpings and asked for seconds. After pie, we could hardly move, and waddled to the back porch. Even Andy got some scraps. Mom let us off the hook for doing dishes, because Dad volunteered to give her a hand. Boy, he saved our lives without a doubt. I don't think that Jack and I could have made it if we'd had to dry all those dishes and put them away.

The three of us all relaxed while the sun went down. Andy loved to stretch out on the cement in the evening. The temperature changes quite a bit when the sun sets in Laredo. I guess there is hardly any humidity, and then, for some reason, there always seems to be a nice breeze.

Anyway, we stayed out there until it was almost time for bed. When we walked into our bedroom, my walkie-talkie rang. I picked it up. "Hello."

"This is Victoria, Eddie. I just thought I'd check in with you so you could think about what I saw after I got back to the school."

"What did you see?"

"I decided to wait around the front to see who was driving the Border Patrol van. He was a different driver. He seemed pretty casual, he's the regular one I think, and at least he spoke normal Mexican Spanish." She let that sink in a minute.

"So you didn't see the guy with the funny accent from Pedro's truck."

"No, he only seems to stop by in the morning."

"Well, maybe you can see if he shows up before you head on over to Cody's. I may not think about this too much tonight, I want to think about our flight tomorrow."

"Yeah, me, too," she said. "Well, good night."

"Good night, Victoria. See you in the morning."

"What did she want?" Jack said, yawning. "She just wanted to pass along that she didn't see that odd-ball driver, just the regular one was there."

"She wanted to bother you with that? Boy, girls are nuts."

"Well, she just wanted to let us know in case we wanted to think about it tonight."

"Well I don't."

"Okay, good night."

Andy curled up in his serious sleeping position. I had just about drifted off when Jack whispered. "Darn Victoria, now she's got me thinking about it. I was going to dream about flying—nuts."

I didn't even answer. I just turned over and went to sleep.

_____

When we got up the next morning, Mom decided to drive us to the base. She said she worried about us when we got too excited—that we might show good judgement when we were riding our bikes. I started to tell her it wasn't that way, but I didn't. She wouldn't have believed me anyway. Since she was driving, I called Victoria to tell her we would pick her up. That would give her longer to see if a strange driver showed up in the van and switched with the one from Pedro's truck. We had cereal and toast, probably because it was quick. I wished Mom had made bacon and eggs, and skipped driving. Oh, well.

When we got to the school, Victoria was sitting on the steps. Mom pulled over, and she jumped in. She just said good morning and that kind of stuff until Mom dropped us off at Cody's office. "What happened?" Jack and I asked simultaneously, after we were alone.

"I was sitting there when the van pulled up. The driver got out and opened the back doors like usual. Then Pedro's truck drove up and the driver got out. He was the same guy with the funny accent that I had seen the other day. He looked at the other driver for a minute, and then got back in his truck. The window was open, so I could see him making a call on a cell-phone. Then he put down the phone and left. He didn't drop off coke or anything."

Just then Luis walked up. "What's up?" he questioned. Victoria filled him in. "Well, at least the guy is still here. We'll see tomorrow if he goes out to Tarantula—that will be a dead give away." We all nodded, and entered the office.

"Hi, Cowboys. You to Sweetheart," he gave Victoria a wink. "I've got the Staggerwing sitting out in front of the Lair. Why don't you guys amble on down there while I get a few things I need for the trip. Luis, why don't you brief them and decide on the seating arrangement."

"Okay, Cody," we said hurrying out the door.

"Last one's there is a male tarantula," Jack said, running toward the hanger like crazy. "Which one of you is going to get eaten up? Ha. Ha."

None of us ran. "Watch out, Jack," Victoria hollered, "The female might be waiting for you by the plane." Jack slowed down pretty quick, and ended up walking with us at the end. I'm not sure what spooked him. It was probably Victoria. I think he believed that she could do anything she set her mind to—even voodoo.

Boy, the Staggerwing looked soooo neat in the morning light. The aircraft's shiny surface seemed to reflect each little ray of sunlight as it danced across the yellow paint, causing little rainbow-like flashes to appear here and there. "That's the prettiest airplane I've ever seen," Victoria said for the umpteenth time. But that was okay, because we all agreed with her.

I talked with Luis and Jack while Victoria was walking around the airplane. "Why don't we put Victoria in the co-pilot's seat—at least for the flight up to San Antonio?" Everyone agreed. "Okay, that's settled. Who gets it on the way back?" We played rocks, paper, and scissors. I beat them in only three tries. At last, I finally, won something. Up till now, Jack had almost won every flip we'd made. Maybe my luck was changing.

Five minutes later, Cody showed up. He tossed a leather navigators bag in the small luggage compartment, and hopped in the left seat. We were all strapped in by that time, and eager to go. Cody flipped on the battery switch and made a quick instrument check. Then he hollered, clear, and hit the start switch. The prop turned over a couple of times and then the engine came alive. Smoke billowed from the twin exhausts until the engine revved up, then it settled down a bit, turning with the sound of quiet power. Cody let it idle for a couple of minutes and then called the tower. "Laredo, triple nickel, how do you read?"

"Roger, five five five, I read you loud and clear. Cleared to taxi runway three six zero, altimeter two niner niner one, call number one.

"Roger, Laredo." He looked around at everybody, "Everyone buckled up? Here we go, Cowboys."

He pushed up the throttle and the aircraft surged ahead, like it was eager to get in the sky where it belonged. We taxied pretty fast, and were soon in the number one position for takeoff. "Laredo, triple nickel number one."

Roger triple nickel, winds zero one five at seven knots, cleared for takeoff, contact Laredo radio when airborne."

Cody set the brakes and revved up the engine. He released the brakes and we seemed to jump down the runway. "Laredo, triple nickel is rolling, see you this afternoon."

"Roger, nickel, have a good trip."

We seemed to be in the air in no time. Cody picked up the gear real quick and held the aircraft low to build up speed. We were racing by the time we got to the end of the runway, and then he zoomed up to five thousand feet. None of us said a thing. I guess we were kind of in shock at the performance of such an old airplane. He let the airspeed build until he reached one hundred and ninety-five miles per hour. Then he pulled back the throttle and trimmed the aircraft. "Would you like to fly for a bit, little lady?" he said, looking at Victoria. She about died then and there. But she recovered with a big gulp and finally said yes.

She took the wheel and the airplane bounced pretty good. Cody calmed her down. "Settle down, little lady, just fly it with your finger tips. Kind of think it into doing what you want, coax it a little. That's how you make an airplane respond. They can tell if you're really in charge, otherwise, they fight you all the way."

She clinched her teeth, and tried again. This time, she was successful. The airplane seemed to know what she wanted it to do after she relaxed. We all looked at each other, sitting in the back, amazed at how she seemed to take control. Pretty soon, she was turning and going up and down, just like she was a trained pilot. "Why, you're a natural pilot if I ever saw one, little lady," Cody said, "I'm going to have to take you up in the PT-22, and teach you a few tricks."

Victoria's lips showed her determination, then she fell for the thing that got most new pilots, us included, she started squeezing the controls. All of a sudden the airplane didn't do what she wanted, and she gave the control back to Cody. "What happened?" she asked, "I thought I was doing fine until…uh…something seemed to happen."

"That's normal, Victoria. Every first time pilot does it. They grip the controls so hard they forget the velvet touch. Don't worry, you're a natural, It won't happen again."

By that time, we were getting pretty close to San Antonio. "I'd better take the controls now; we're getting close to Hondo."

Cody changed the radio and keyed the mike. "Hondo tower, this is Beech five five five, VFR from Laredo, request landing instructions."

"Roger, Beech five five five, cleared VFR approach runway two eight zero, altimeter three zero one two, call three miles."

We had followed highway 35 all the way to Pearsall. When it made a turn to the right, towards San Antonio, we went straight to Hondo. Cody spoke up. "Hondo used to be an old Air Force contract base, used for primary pilot training. There are a lot of commercial outfits that fly out of there since the Air Force left, just like Alamo Air, the outfit we're going to visit today. There aren't many fields left around here anymore that allow multiple approaches and landings. That's why they fly down to Tarantula. They get all the landings they can need without wasting a lot of time, and can practice visual navigation on the way down and back. All the time Cody was descending and lining up with the runway. "Hondo, Beech five five five, three miles."

"Roger, five five five, we have you in sight, cleared to land runway two eight zero, winds light and variable, altimeter three zero one two."

"Roger, Hondo, gear down and checked." Cody really squeaked it on and turned off at mid-field. "Hondo, I'm going over to Alamo Air, thanks for your help."

The tower operator spoke up, "That Staggerwing looks better every time I see it, Cody, you lucky dog."

"That's because my Cowboys keep it in good shape, Hondo. See you about eleven if you're still working."

"I'll be working."

Cody taxied over to a big hanger toward the end of the ramp. There were three Learjet's sitting out front. Cody parked next to the one on the far end, and shut her down. We all thanked him for the ride, and asked him what he wanted us to do. "I'm going in to get a contract signed with the guys in the head office. After that, I thought we might wander around a little and see if we can get you inside one of these little jets."

"That would be terrific, Cody," I said, everyone nodded. We hopped out and followed Cody to an office off the back side of the hanger. He talked with a couple of people, and then handed them a bunch of papers from out of his navigator bag.

He walked back over to us. "Okay Cowboys, I got us permission to snoop around in one of the planes in the hanger—number seven two six. It's down for a periodic inspection, and all of the systems are safetied. I'll come back here afterwards and pick up my papers." We followed him out the door and wandered into the hanger. Wow, there were three more jets parked in there.

"There it is," pointed Luis, "the one in the corner over there." Cody decided to give us a tour of the outside, first. It wasn't a very big airplane, and sat really low to the ground. We had to duck way down to see the landing gear. The engines were mounted on each side of the fuselage near the back, almost to the tail. Heck, they were low enough for us to jump up a little and look inside the intakes and the tail pipes. The tail was mounted high, so we couldn't touch that.

Next we climbed into the aircraft. We entered the cabin by walking up four stairs that were part of the door. The cabin wasn't very big; all of us kids could touch the ceiling. There were six pretty nice seats, four of them were made to swivel, and so they could face a table which pulled out of the floor. The last two seats were near the back, by the lavatory door. To enter the flight deck (you didn't call it a cockpit on this plane), you walked through a little opening between two coat racks. The flight deck was all business. There were a million dials and switches, it seemed, and made me wonder how the pilot could look at them and fly at the same time. The seats were really comfortable and held the pilot in place real good. We each took turns pretending that we were flying—even Victoria. I think she was having the time of her life.

When we had all finished playing jet pilot, we went back toward the office where Cody was going to pick up his signed papers. We decided to wait on a bench over behind some maintenance racks near the office, when we heard a couple of guys talking. I couldn't understand what they were saying, until I realized they were speaking Spanish. Suddenly, Victoria gave us a shush signal, and moved over behind the rack where she could hear better. She motioned for Luis to join her. They both listened until the two men departed out the front of the hanger. They hurried back, both of them talking to each other like mad. "Did you catch that accent?" Victoria asked Luis as they walked up.

"Yes, it was different than I'm used to; there were even a few words I couldn't understand. Is that a South American dialect?"

Victoria nodded, "Yes. It's the same accent as the guy that was driving Pedro's truck." With that comment, we all bristled, and kind of looked around nervous like.

About that time, Cody came out of the office and almost scared us to death, causing us to jump with fright. "What's going on Cowboys? Y'all look like you've seen a ghost." No one said a word. "Well, which one of you is going to tell me?"

Victoria spoke up. "We're just a little nervous, that's all. It's kind of silly—really, it's nothing."

"Okay, gang. Let's head for the plane." After a few paces, he turned to us. "Who ever sits in the right seat on the flight back is going to tell me what in the dickens is going on." He turned and headed off.

I gulped. "Right seat—that's me." I whispered to the gang. "What am I going to say? He'll know if I lie."

Finally, Luis spoke up. "Just tell him the truth, Eddie. He'll find out anyhow, he always does. I don't think he will tell our parents or anything—he's a straight shooter."

"Does Eddie tell him about tomorrow? That we are trying to catch the terrorists red-handed?" Jack thought a second, and then added. "I agree with Luis. I don't think he would rat on us about the theory stuff, but if we tell him we're trying to catch them in the act—that's different."

Well, it was too late now. We were approaching the plane. Cody had already made the preflight and was ready to board. "I'll play it by ear," I whispered to the gang as I let them enter in front of me.

Cody looked over. "So it's you, Eddie. I'll bet you wish you hadn't won the co-pilot's seat now?" he grinned, going on about his business while he started her up.

He had me there. Man, I swear. I thought my luck had changed when I won playing rocks, paper and scissors. No, I realized, I was just as unlucky as ever.

We took off and headed south. I was beginning to think he had forgotten about asking me why we had been so jumpy. "Want to fly, Eddie?" Cody asked.

I jumped at the chance. "Sure, Cody."

"Okay, you've got it." He let me take the controls. I tried to remember everything he said about being light on the controls. I was even learning a little bit about how to trim the aircraft, so the controls didn't pull in one direction or another. I started making little turns back and forth, and then added a little dive and zoom to the pattern as I changed directions. Just when I was feeling really comfortable, he spoke up. "Well, Eddie. When are you going to spill the beans?"

Of course that caused me to over-control everything, but he didn't take over the controls, he just sat there. I tried to relax and eventually got things back to straight and level. Then Cody remarked. "It's kind of like walking and chewing gum at the same time, Eddie. Just let the airplane do the work, and you can talk. Now, what got you guys so all fired spooked up?"

"Well," I started slowly, "Luis has told you a little bit about the guy driving Pedro's truck, right?" He nodded, still not touching the controls. "Did he tell you that Victoria is kind of a language expert, that she can tell different dialects and stuff?" He nodded again. "Well she overheard the guy driving the truck, and he speaks South American Spanish."

"So what does that have to do with y'all being scared?"

I was still working to keep the airplane level. "Well, the terrorist that was caught in Dallas by the FBI was a member of the Shining Path terrorist group. They are from Peru, and have connections with some Arab terrorists. The guy told the FBI that he entered the country through Laredo. We think we know how he did it." Cody looked up, really surprised. "We think he was picked up at Tarantula by one of those Learjets. Then, while you were in the office, Victoria heard two Learjet pilots speaking Spanish with South American dialects. We believe they could be planning to pick up the guy driving Pedro's truck tomorrow." My knuckles were white by this time—I think Cody noticed.

"I've got it." He trimmed up the aircraft and then looked over. "You mean you were planning to catch these guys in the act?" He looked around at everyone. "What in the world were you planning to do if they actually did pick him up? Shoot them with a water pistol or something?"

Victoria couldn't stand it any more and entered the conversation. "We were just trying to find out if our theory was right. We weren't going to try to stop them or do anything stupid." That brought on a steady stream of talk from all of us.

Cody yelled. "Hold it, everybody. I need to think this over." He sat there for a minute. "Cowboys, we need a plan. Let me think about it while I put this baby on the ground. Then we can talk about it in my office." He started a rapid descent. "Laredo tower, this is triple-nickel, requesting a VFR approach."

"Hi, Cody. Cleared to land runway one eight zero, altimeter two niner niner two, call one mile final."

Three minutes later. "Laredo, the nickel is one mile for a full stop."

"Cleared to land, runway one eight zero, winds one nine five at two knots, contact ground control when clear."

"Roger, Laredo, gear down and locked." The landing was smooth as glass and we quickly taxied to the Lair. We hurriedly buttoned up the plane and went to Cody's office.

We all pulled up a seat and waited for Cody to speak. He looked at each one of us carefully. "Have you told me <u>everything</u> that's going on?" We looked at each other.

Finally, Luis spoke up, kind of red-faced. "Not <u>every</u> little detail, I guess, but almost everything."

Cody sat back in his chair. "I got all the rest of the day, people. Someone fill me in. I want to know <u>everything</u>."

It must have taken us an hour to spill the beans, as Cody had put it. Afterwards, he got up and paced around for a couple of minutes, then took his seat. "Now here's what were going to do. I can see that y'all have a lot of loose ends here. First, you have never actually proved that the terrorists are entering the country on that Border Patrol van. But it makes a lot of sense, considering the way Pedro's truck keeps showing up, and the fact that these guys have access to the government compound is even more bothersome. Secondly, you have no idea who the burglar was out there at Tarantula. But again, you have something to tie him to the terrorists; the paper written in Arabic says he might be connected. Third, you don't have any proof, other than the fact that a couple of pilots for Alamo Air were speaking in a South American dialect. There is nothing to show that someone at Alamo is sympathetic with the terrorists and is helping them by picking them up at Tarantula. You simply have no proof." He sat back and was quiet, doing some heavy thinking. He stood up. "Cowboys, I like your theory, and I think you might be correct. But if we told the FBI, I don't think they could make a legal case for any of this, and our suspects probably have cover-stories ten miles long. Therefore, we are going to act on our own. We are going to test your theory to see if we can get some hard proof. Then, we can turn it over to the experts. Agreed?"

We all jumped up and danced around. "Hold it, Cowboys, aren't we forgetting something? We stood there dumbfounded while Cody reached into his drawer and pulled out a light blue shirt. "We've got a new member of Cody's Lair—actually she is our first, Cowgirl."

He handed it to Victoria.

She stood there with her mouth open as she looked at the shirt. Jack hollered, "Put it on, Victoria."

She turned a little red. "I can't here. Wait a minute," she said, running toward the bathroom. Pretty soon she came back with the shirt on. "How does it look," she said with the biggest smile I have ever seen.

"It looks great," we all said, "Welcome to Cody's Lair, Cowgirl."

Cody said he had some stuff to do, and he'd talk to us in the morning, just before we went to Tarantula. The four of us left, and headed over to the school where Mom was going to pick us up.

After we were out of sight, Cody picked up the phone. "Jim Matthews, please. When will he be back? Okay, will you please tell him to call Cody over at the Lone Star Flying Service? Tell him it's urgent. Tell him I'll wait here until he calls."

CHAPTER FOURTEEN

Jack and I didn't sleep much that night. I guess we were worried about what might happen at Tarantula. Andy didn't have any trouble, however, he never did. We dressed in our required outfits: jeans, boots, long sleeved shirts, stupid hats, and gobs of sunscreen.

Mom seemed really happy, and was just singing away in the kitchen when we walked in. "Oh, good-morning, you two. How would you like your eggs, scrambled, over easy, or poached?"

I was kind of surprised she was so happy. I guess that she and Dad were getting along really well, or something like that, it seems to happen every once in a while.

"What's poached?" Jack asked.

"They are kind of like soft-boiled, only they are cooked and served out of the shell," Mom said, happily.

"I think I'd like to try one of those, Mrs. Matthews."

"Me too," I added quickly.

"We're also having sausage and biscuits," Mom said, still humming away.

"Biscuits! Wow! I haven't had biscuits since I can remember," Jack said, dancing around. "Oh, boy."

"Yeah, great, Mom. What's the occasion?" I asked, wondering if I had missed something important.

"Nothing special, I just decided to have biscuits and honey, I always loved that combination. And they go great with sausage," she added quickly.

Jack and I sat down and waited for Mom to finish, and then we jumped up and got our plates. The biscuits were huge. Mom served the poached egg on one half of a biscuit, and gave us each two patties of sausage. Then she put a plate of extra biscuits on the table. We had butter, jam, and honey. This was one of the all-time greatest breakfasts I had ever had. Jack agreed, when he could talk, his mouth was chewing most of the time.

Fortunately, we didn't have to get to Tarantula until eleven o'clock. After breakfast, we helped dry the dishes, and then just sat around in back for a while. Andy tried to get us interested in investigating Oscars burrow, but we didn't bite. Hey, that's a joke—didn't bite, get it? Anyway, we decided to leave about nine-thirty, so we would be there in plenty of time to ride out with the fire crew. Of course, we wanted to see if the rest of the gang had heard anything new. It was kind of hot when we left, and we were sweating away by the time we got there. It felt good to go into Cody's office where it was air conditioned.

Everyone got there by ten. None of us had anything new to offer. Cody spoke up. "Okay, Cowboys, I want you to be careful, and, what ever you do, you are <u>not</u> to challenge anyone—for any reason." He made us promise. Then he added, "I want you to call me on your walkie-talkie if you think that anything might be going wrong—anything at all, do you understand?" We all promised, again, and went out to wait for the fire truck. The only one of us to have a lunch was Victoria, and that got us talking. She said her Aunt made her bring it just in case she got hungry. "I quit arguing with her years ago," she said, kind of nonchalantly, "My Aunt is as strict as my Mom."

"Well she's your mom's sister isn't she?" Jack exclaimed, "She should be strict."

Victoria nodded, "I think she is even stricter. She doesn't have any kids—that makes her worse—she doesn't understand us." We all nodded that we understood about grown-ups, and how they reacted to things like this. We all knew that parents over-reacted to everything that involved us.

"We need to be left alone more," I said, "Like Cody treats us. He doesn't go nuts anytime we say anything."

Everyone agreed. I think we all felt we could trust Cody. It was different than our parents. Of course we could trust our parents most of the time; it was just that they seemed to over-react to everything they didn't think up in the first place. "Cody trusts us," Luis said. "Other wise he would have told our parents or somebody, and we wouldn't be allowed to go to Tarantula today." It was just a fact, we all trusted him completely.

The fire truck pulled up besides us and we jumped in. The guys were a little bit quiet today, so we didn't sing or anything on the way to Tarantula.

Everything was routine about the opening. The runway was checked and the fire truck moved to their parking place. We stocked the refrigerator, turned on the power and checked in with Laredo tower. Then we dispersed: Luis and Jack stood by in the mobile, while Victoria and I positioned ourselves north of the runway, at a shady spot in the arroyo where we'd released Porky. All we could do now was to wait for an instructor from Alamo Air to show up, and the operation could start.

After a while a Cessna 172 showed up and started shooting landings. We were getting tired and bored just sitting there waiting for the Learjet, so we started looking around for a place to hide that was closer to the pad near the end of the runway. When we moved out, we spooked a couple of rattlesnakes and a few tarantulas, but they didn't cause us any trouble. During our search for a hiding place, we saw a big old mesquite tree grove over to our right, and thought it might be a good place to observe from.

Just as we started sneaking across an open place, we spotted two or three Javelina. They were snorting away, rooting around out in the open between us and the Mesquite grove. We squatted down behind some sage brush and watched them for a couple of minutes, deciding what to do. They kept getting closer and closer to a big mesquite tree when someone began throwing rocks at them. Victoria punched me on the shoulder, "Eddie, there is a man there under that tree. See him?"

I looked closer. "Yeah, I see him. He's throwing rocks at those pigs." Suddenly it dawned on us. It must be the terrorist waiting for his ride. We looked at each other and kind of shivered.

"Come on," Victoria said, after we settled down, "Let's move over to the west a little bit. That will put him on the side away from the runway where he'll be looking." Good idea, I thought, as we sneaked along on our hands and knees. We found a small arroyo that would give us a little cover. When we got there, we almost fell in a small cave on the side of the bank. It didn't seem very big, and we couldn't really see inside. Thinking it might be a Javelina den, we moved on a little farther until we found a spot that had a good view of both the tree and the parking pad.

"Do you think we'll be safe here?" Victoria asked, taking a peek from behind a big bush.

"Sure," I said, "Were just going to watch. That guy won't know we're back here. He'll be concentrating on the Learjet." She nodded, but didn't look real satisfied with my theory. "Besides," I added, "As soon as the Learjet gets here, Luis and Jack are going to move over to the fire truck. Then, we can talk to them over the walkie-talkie, and tell him about the guy behind the mesquite tree." She nodded again, this time seeming to have a little more confidence.

Suddenly, my walkie-talkie rang. "Eddie," this is Jack. Can you hear me?"

I hunkered down behind the bank and put my walkie-talkie into my giant hat, hoping to muffle the sound. "Hi, Jack," I whispered, feeling stupid, lying there talking into my hat. "Where is the Learjet? Is it coming?"

"Yes, they just checked in. I'm outside the mobile now. As soon as the instructor shows up, we are going to move over to the fire truck."

"Jack, listen close. The terrorist is waiting in a little grove of mesquite trees near the pad. You might want to call Cody when you get out of there. I shouldn't be talking to you, the guy might hear me. We're just west of him, about two hundred feet away. I better shut up. Bye." I turned to Victoria after I turned off the walkie-talkie. "Do you think that guy heard me?"

She shook her head, "No, I don't think he did, at least he didn't look around or anything. What did Jack want?"

"He said the Learjet is almost here, and they will move right after they drop off the instructor." She nodded that she understood.

After what seemed like an hour, we heard the jet. It landed and rolled out all the way to our end of the runway and turned around on the pad close to us. Then it taxied back down the runway to the mobile, where it dropped off someone—an instructor, I guess. We saw the guy in the trees, wave as the jet passed by on the way to the mobile, making us certain that something was going to happen. Pretty soon the jet took off, and started shooting touch-and-go landings. After five landings, the Learjet made a full stop landing, and was taxiing toward the parking pad. Victoria punched me in the ribs. "The guy is coming this way," she said, her eyes big as saucers. We ducked down as much as possible. There wasn't much cover, so I left Victoria behind a big bush and tried to hide behind some sage brush on the other side of the arroyo.

The guy headed right for the little cave we had spotted earlier and reached inside. He pulled out two black suitcases. He looked around, checking that everything was okay, then picked up the cases, and started to crawl out of the arroyo. Just then, I felt something on my hand. I looked over and saw a humongous scorpion, his tail poised and ready to strike. Without thinking I jerked up my hand and the critter went flying off into the arroyo.

That's when the terrorist saw me. He pulled out a gun and pointed it at me. "You! Boy! What are you doing here?" he asked, coming closer.

I don't know why, but I jumped up and screamed bloody-murder. Then, I turned and started to run away. I was thinking that I was going to get shot when I heard Victoria. "Don't shoot," She screeched, standing up, *"No Tirar, por favor."* I tripped when I started to change directions and fell to the ground, rolling over a couple of times. When the dust settled, I realized that I was still alive, and lying in a shallow ditch. I stuck my head up and took a look.

The man had turned his gun toward Victoria. "Pick up those cases and head for the plane," he said, his voice sounding cold and serious. "You're coming with me."

"No!" Victoria said. "Pick them up yourself. I'm not coming," she replied defiantly. He pointed the gun at her, and, at the last minute, shot at the ground right next to her feet. Her eyes were full of terror. "Okay," she said quietly, inching her way toward the cases. By the time she got close to him I could see she was shaking.

I keyed my walkie-talkie and screamed—HELP! Then I dropped it on the ground and jumped up. "Let her go," I shouted. "I'll carry the cases." I started walking slowly toward the man.

Everything was kind of like slow motion from then on. I could see someone at the plane motioning to the man and screaming something. Victoria had stopped and was just standing there, shaking. Everything seemed to be kind of quiet—spooky like. I heard the fire truck start up and roar down the runway, and saw it stop in the middle, blocking the Learjet.

Just as I was almost there, about ten feet from Victoria, her walkie-talkie started to ring. That's when the man turned his attention to her again. The guy retreated slowly, looking back and forth between us, trying to decide what to do. He must have decided on Victoria, who was only about five feet from him, because he pointed the gun right at her head. I thought he was going to shoot her for sure.

Then I heard a squeal, and saw a little black Javelina charging the terrorist. The man looked around just as the Javelina gored him on his leg. He let out a yell, and was moaning when he fell over, causing his gun to fire. Then, suddenly, there seemed to be a hundred Javelina all around him, all trying to get him. He was screaming his head off when I heard a helicopter.

I ran and grabbed Victoria by the hand and pulled her down the arroyo, trying to get as far as possible away from the guy. The noise from the helicopter was about the only thing I could hear. I felt the rotor-wash as the chopper landed just on the other side of us, toward the Learjet. I looked around. A bunch of soldiers in black uniforms jumped out and were running every which way. Right away, two guys grabbed the terrorist, yanked him up, and dragged him off toward the helicopter.

Then I saw Dad and Cody. They were running toward us for all they were worth. We stopped and waited for them, both of us still dazed from what had happened. They gave us big hugs and checked us out for injuries, then started to lead us back toward the helicopter. "Hold it, Dad," I said, pointing to the arroyo, "We need to bring the cases," I pointed back at the two black bags. "My walkie-talkie is there somewhere, too." Cody found the walkie-talkie, and grabbed the bags while Dad led Victoria and me to safety.

By the time we had caught our breaths, Luis and Jack came running up. "Are you all-right?" they hollered, looking worried. I shrugged my shoulders, honestly not knowing how I was. Victoria just stood there. Luis helped Cody with the cases, while Dad guided Victoria and me toward the helicopter. Then, for some reason, I stopped and looked around, back where we had been. I saw a little Javelina watching us leave from under a bush. I wondered if it was Porky. Deep in my heart I just knew it had to be—thanks, Porky, I thought.

Victoria had just about stopped shaking when a second chopper landed. Dad motioned for us to get on board. We climbed in the back, sat down next to each other, and buckled our seatbelts. After we took off, Victoria took my hand. We just looked at each other for a minute. That's when I knew we were going to be best friends for life.

Mom, Mrs. Porter, and Mrs. Rodriguez were waiting for us when we landed at Dad's compound. They about squeezed the life out of all of us. We went into Dad's office and had a coke while we learned all about what had happened.

It seemed like everybody talked at once, for a while, telling us how dangerous it had been. I guess it was then when it finally started sinking in, and Victoria and I started shaking all over for the second time.

———————————

By the time everybody quit talking, we learned that the Special Forces team on the first helicopter had captured the terrorist and four of his cohorts—the two pilots we had seen at Alamo Air, and the other two crew-members. They also recovered a list of names of the whole terrorist ring, most of which were in the Dallas/Ft. Worth area. Someone said the FBI was already rounding them up.

One of the suitcases they recovered was full of money, almost two million dollars in cash. The other suitcase contained thousands of documents and a metal vial filled with some kind of bacteriological stuff—a weapon of mass destruction an FBI Agent called it. Apparently, the gunk was destined for the lake that feeds the Dallas water supply. The experts said that it was pretty scary to think about what might have happened.

The FBI also arrested the guy who had bought Pedro's business, as well as four of his drivers—all working for the terrorists. Even now, they were in the process of cleaned up the mess within the Border Patrol. I guess there were quite a few guys who were taking bribes, mainly drivers who were subsidizing their income by letting a bad guy take their place once in a while, figuring they would never get caught.

What a day. All of us were really beat and ready to go home. Finally, Cody explained that he had let my Dad in on the whole operation yesterday evening after we had left. Dad was the one who had set up the Special Forces team just in case any of us got in trouble—which they didn't believe would happen. Of course, they had a lot of explaining to do with the FBI and the CI...I mean that government agency he worked for. Anyway, the Agency big shots said they would have never solved the problem without us kids, and that we were all considered heroes. We were all thankful for that, otherwise our parents would have grounded us forever.

————————

At last, we were left alone for a while and able to talk. We still felt kind of scared, mainly because we hadn't realized how much danger we had faced. After each of us had told his part of the story, we all were able to relax.

After a while Cody walked over to us. He tipped his hat to Victoria. "Sweetie," then he turned to the rest of us, "All of you Cowboys, I want to tell you how sorry I am that I had to break your confidence. I'm hoping that you'll forgive me for that. At first, I didn't think you would be in danger, but I just had one of those feelings that I couldn't shake. Anyway, I called Mr. Matthews, and we talked over the whole scheme. He understood the need to sure about it, in spite of the danger potential, and played along with me. He looked right at me, "I can tell you, Eddie, your Dad's a good one." He looked at the others, "He had confidence in <u>all</u> of you, or he wouldn't have done what he did."

Cody paused for a second. "All of your parents are as proud as punch. Your mom, too, Jack. Mrs. Matthews has already talked with her—and Victoria; she talked with your mom and dad too. He went over and put his arm around Luis, giving him a big squeeze. "Buddy, your mom thinks you walk on water, and are the reincarnation of your dad—I think so too. Carlos would have been so proud of you. It was amazing that you had the foresight to have the fire truck block that Learjet. <u>All</u> of you showed a lot of courage today." He kind of paused for a minute and took a deep breath.

He started to leave and then turned. "I guess it's okay for me to spill the beans, and tell you that Victoria's and Jack's folks are on the way from Florida as we speak. I think they are already on a plane headed this way, courtesy of the CIA." He checked his watch. "They should be here pretty soon, if I'm not mistaken." He stood back and just looked at us for a minute. "And for me, I couldn't be prouder that you are all members of Cody's Lair." He wiped a tear from his eye and walked away, leaving us alone.

After he left, we made a circle and held hands, just like we did when we took our oath of secrecy, only this time we thanked each other for being special friends and vowed to remain best friends forever.

Before long, a Gulfstream parked on the ramp outside, and dropped off Victoria's folks and Mrs. Davis. Then we learned, that they brought them here so they could witness some kind of special ceremony the government was having for us the next day. We were all dumbfounded, but were happy to see that the special people in our lives were here for what ever was going to happen.

———————————

Finally, we went home. Jack's mom came with us. She was going to stay in our extra bedroom while she was here. Victoria, her folks, and Mrs. Porter left for their school apartment, and Luis left arm and arm with his mom. It had been quite a day. After thinking about it, I guess we were all lucky to be alive.

Andy gave Jack and I a special greeting when we walked in the house. Somehow, he always seemed to know when something extraordinary had happened. Jack and I took a shower and put on some clean clothes. I don't even remember who went first in the shower; I think we had finally gotten over flipping.

After we came out of the bedroom, Jack's mom took him to the side and hugged the daylights out of him, and then she started scolding him for putting himself in such terrible danger. Pretty soon Mom caught me, and I got more of the same. It seemed like all we could say was: Yes, Mom—Yes, Mother—No, Mom—Never again, Mom—stuff like that. Finally Dad came in and kind of settled things down.

Pretty soon the moms stopped lecturing, and were in the kitchen cooking up a storm. Mmmm, I could smell fried chicken, mashed potatoes and gravy, peas, and home made biscuits. Jack, Andy, and me, were all licking our chops as we stood there. I didn't realize how much the kind of heavy adventure we'd been living whetted our appetites—no wonder we were taller.

After dinner, which was about the best we had ever eaten, Jack and I went to bed early. Andy was already waiting for us, and had fixed his pillow. We laid there in the dark for a little bit before saying anything.

"Eddie?" Jack whispered.

"Yeah?"

"Were you scared when that guy pointed a gun at you?"

"Sure."

"Were you as scared as Victoria?"

"How in the heck would I know, Jack?"

"Well, you were there, weren't you?"

"Sure, but that doesn't mean that I know how she felt. I mean, I was almost more scared when that creep pointed his gun at her head. I think it's supposed to be that way—for guys, at least. Men are supposed to worry about women more than themselves, I think. That's what they do in the movies and in books and stuff."

"Maybe that was why I was so scared—even though I wasn't down there with you guys. I guess I was thinking about Victoria."

"There was plenty of <u>scare</u> for everybody today, Jack. Everybody says we were lucky—especially our moms."

"I think we were pretty smart, too, Eddie. Cody said so, didn't he?"

"Yeah. We did pretty good, I guess. I don't think we should do it again—at least not right away. Know what I mean?"

"Yeah, I know what you mean. I hope I'm never that scared again in my whole life."

"Me, too."

Yawn. "Well, good night, Eddie." There was quiet for a while. "Bet I know what you're dreaming about, Eddie."

"Shut up."

We both woke up early. It was just starting to get light. It was even too early for Andy, who had smushed down on his pillow pretending to be sound asleep. Jack and I threw on some clothes and sneaked out to the kitchen. We got us a glass of orange juice and sat out on the back porch to watch the sunrise. It was real pretty. Bunches of yellowish-orange rays kind of poked through the big trees next door, and danced around on our lawn. I got to thinking that it was hard to catch a good sunrise like we had this morning, most of the time it just gets light all at once.

We had finished our juice and just started to go inside when we heard Oscar scratching the tile as he left his burrow. He peeked around the corner at us and then just went on his merry way down the fence searching for bugs or something. I guess he knew that Andy wasn't with us.

Mom and Mrs. Davis had gotten up by now and were messing around in the kitchen, trying to decide what to fix. I had a feeling it was going to be good, since this was a special day. We got kissed and hugged like mad when we walked in the kitchen. I decided it must be the price you had to pay when you became heroes like us. Afterwards, of course, they sent us in to brush our teeth and comb our hair—they never stopped being moms. We did talk them out of putting on our dress clothes, however, because it was so early and we reminded them that we would probably slop something messy on our shirts at breakfast. Anyway, I felt pretty good, although my left knee was a little sore from falling down in that arroyo.

I finally got Andy up, fed him, and took him for a short walk. When we got back, Dad was up and the women had decided on Belgian Waffles with strawberries. Boy, were those waffles good. I don't know how many Jack and I ate, Mom just kept passing out those little pie-shaped quarters as fast as we could down them. Good thing we hadn't dressed up, because both Jack and I had big strawberry juice marks all down our fronts.

We put on our gray dress pants and white short sleeved shirts. The moms made us wear ties. Naturally, we looked almost alike. "Did they think we were twins?

Dad drove us to the base theater, where the ceremony was supposed to take place. There were satellite trucks all over the place, and there were lots of people with cameras taking pictures of us. There were reporters, too. None of us could walk without someone sticking a mike in our mouths. We met up with Victoria and her group when we got to the front walk. It was awful, everybody was pushing and shoving. Finally, a group of special police surrounded us and ushered us inside, keeping all of the reporters away.

Luis was already inside. His mom had made him wear a tie, too. We all got together and said hello. Victoria really looked pretty. She had on a yellow dress with little flowers on it, and someone had fixed her hair so it didn't bush out in back. I think she also had on some stuff on her face to make her look pink—she even smelled good. Anyway, she didn't look like she did yesterday when that guy stuck a gun in her face.

Without warning, some guy in charge of things ushered us up on the stage next to a podium and sat us down, separate from our folks. I looked around. There were American flags everywhere—and almost as many Texas flags. There were lots and lots of people in the seats out front, and flash-bulbs were flashing all over the place. Finally, the curtain behind us went up and a band started playing. They were Marines, and they played really loud. Finally some people in suits walked on the stage and everybody murmured. Then the band played our National Anthem. We all jumped up and placed our hands over our hearts. I sang along with the music, so did everybody else. Then it was over.

It was real quiet, and then someone said over the loud-speaker, "Ladies and Gentlemen, the President of the United States." The band played something else. Then we saw President Bush walk out on the stage. He was wearing cowboy boots, probably because he had been at his ranch in Crawford. He came right over to us, smiling away, and even called us by name when he shook our hands. Wow! Then he went back to the podium and made a little speech. I don't remember much about what he said, but it was about us. I think we all turned red in the face. I could see Mom in the front row, crying her eyes out. Dad was wiping his eyes too. Finally the President motioned for us to come over by him. We all went over and stood in a row so he could present us with gold medals of something or other. The President put the ribbon around our necks and said congratulations and some other stuff.

Someone stuck a microphone in front of Jack, who was on the end of our row. He said, "Thank you Mr. President. We were happy to help." The crowd cheered.

I'm not sure if I said anything or not—or if anybody else did. All I know is that I had a big lump in my throat and really felt proud.

Well, that's the end of the story about my great adventure this summer. I couldn't have believed it would have turned out this way when I learned about coming here to Laredo last April. I wasn't sure what was going to happen next in my life, but I don't think it could be any more exciting—Unless, it's when the four of us Cody's Cowboys all get together again.

ABOUT THE AUTHOR

The author grew up during World War II. He lived in an almost fatherless neighborhood with his boyhood friends; consequently searching for heroes, he found them in books and in the newsreels at Saturday matinees. His first "real" hero was an Army Air Corps pilot who gave him his first flight in an open cockpit trainer. He introduced Dick to aerobatics and taught him the joys of playing with the clouds; the young boy left part of his soul in the sky, providing him with his first life quest. He became an Air Force fighter pilot and served his country for thirty-three years. After retirement, he recalled the stories and events that influenced him during his formative years and decided to becoming a teller of stories, so that he might positively inspire others to follow their own dreams.

Printed in the United States
40365LVS00005B/187-288